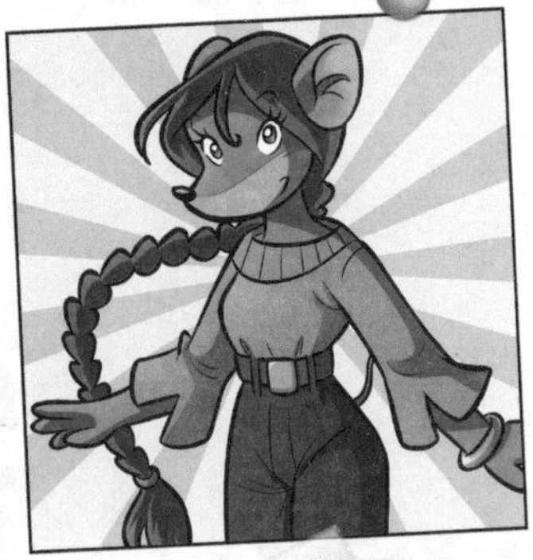

PAULINA
is thoughtful and responsible. Sometimes she's like a second mom to her friends.

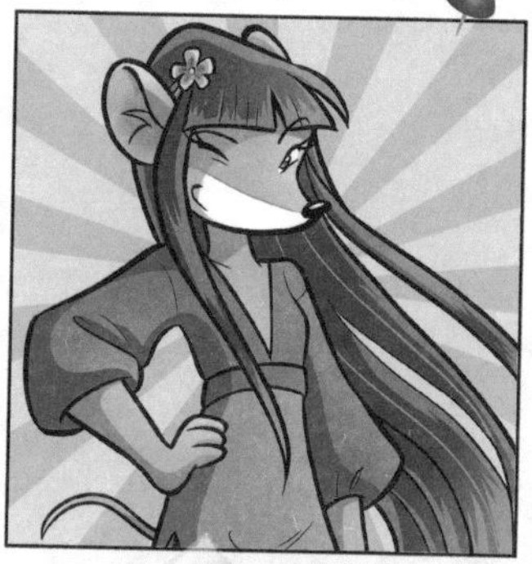

Violet
often quotes ancient Chinese proverbs. She can calm the whole group with her wisdom.

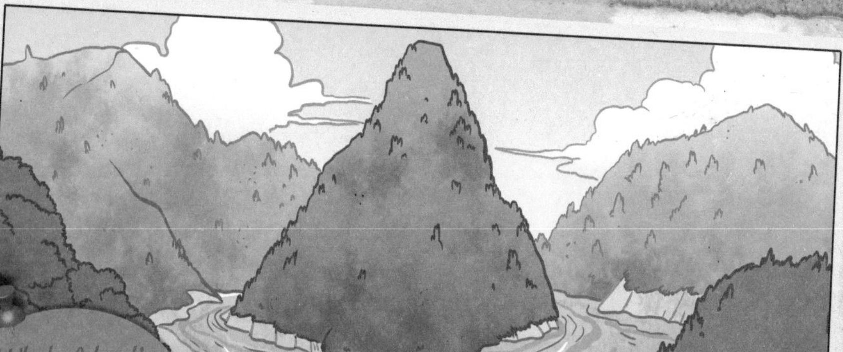

Whale Island's
dam at the top of the mountain is opened every spring to bring the river in the forest to life.

Thea Stilton

PAPERCUTZ™

Thea Stilton

Graphic Novels Available from

PAPERCUTZ™

All-new, full-color Graphic Novel
Thea Stilton
THE SECRET OF WHALE ISLAND
PAPERCUTZ

Graphic Novel #1
"The Secret of Whale Island"

All-new, full-color Graphic Novel
Thea Stilton
REVENGE OF THE LIZARD CLUB
MOUSEFORD RACE
PAPERCUTZ

Graphic Novel #2
"Revenge of the Lizard Club"

All-new, full-color Graphic Novel
Thea Stilton
THE TREASURE OF THE VIKING SHIP
PAPERCUTZ

Graphic Novel #3
"The Treasure of the Viking Ship"

All-new, full-color Graphic Novel
Thea Stilton
CATCHING THE GIANT WAVE
PAPERCUTZ

Graphic Novel #4
"Catching the Giant Wave"

All-new, full-color Graphic Novel
Thea Stilton
THE SECRET OF THE WATERFALL IN THE WOODS
PAPERCUTZ

Graphic Novel #5
"The Secret of the Waterfall in the Woods"

COMING SOON

Thea Stilton
THE THEA SISTERS
MYSTERY AT SEA
PAPERCUTZ

Graphic Novel #6
"Mystery at Sea"

THEA STILTON graphic novels are available for $9.99 each only in hardcover. Available from booksellers everywhere. You can also order online from www.papercutz.com. Or call 1-800-886-1223, Monday through Friday, 9 – 5 EST. MC, Visa, and AmEx accepted. To order by mail, please add $4.00 for postage and handling for first book ordered, $1.00 for each additional book and make check payable to NBM Publishing. Send to: Papercutz, 160 Broadway, Suite 700, East Wing, New York, NY 10038.

THEA STILTON graphic novels are also available digitally wherever e-books are sold.

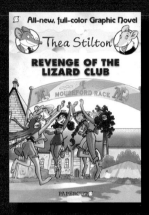

Thea Stilton

THE SECRET OF THE WATERFALL IN THE WOODS

By Thea Stilton

PAPERCUTZ™

New York

THEA STILTON #5
THE SECRET OF THE WATERFALL IN THE WOODS
Geronimo Stilton and Thea Stilton names, characters and related indicia and all images are copyright,
trademark and exclusive license of Atlantyca S.p.A.
All rights reserved.
The moral right of the author has been asserted.

Text by Thea Stilton
Original Cover by Ryan Jampole (artist) and JayJay Jackson (colorist)
Project Supervision by Alessandra Berello (Atlantyca S.p.A.)
Script by Francesco Savino and Leonardo Favia
Translation by Nanette McGuinness
Art by Ryan Jampole
Color by Mindy Indy
With the assistance of Matt Herms
Lettering by Wilson Ramos, Jr. and Grace Lu

© Atlantyca S.p.A. – via Leopardi 8, 20123 Milano, Italia – foreignrights@atlantyca.it
© 2015 Papercutz, 160 Broadway, Suite 700, East Wing, New York, NY 10038, for this Work in English language.

Based on an original idea by Elisabetta Dami

www.geronimostilton.com

Stilton is the name of a famous English cheese. It is a registered trademark of the
Stilton Cheese Makers' Association. For more information go to www.stiltoncheese.com

Papercutz books may be purchased for business or promotional use. For information on bulk purchases
please contact Macmillan Corporate and Premium Sales Department at (800) 221-7945 x5442.

Production – Dawn Guzzo
Production Coordinator – Jeff Whitman
Editor – Carol M. Burrell
Associate Editor – Bethany Bryan
Jim Salicrup
Editor-in-Chief

ISBN: 978-1-62991-288-2

Printed in China.
December 2015 by WKT Co. LTD.
3/F Phase 1 Leader Industrial Centre
188 Texaco Road, Tsuen Wan, N.T.
Hong Kong

Distributed by Macmillan
First Printing

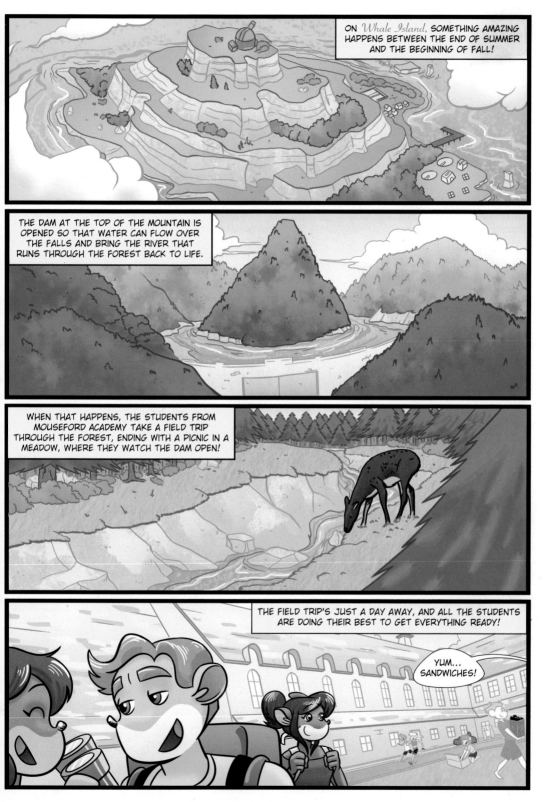

ON *Whale Island*, SOMETHING AMAZING HAPPENS BETWEEN THE END OF SUMMER AND THE BEGINNING OF FALL!

THE DAM AT THE TOP OF THE MOUNTAIN IS OPENED SO THAT WATER CAN FLOW OVER THE FALLS AND BRING THE RIVER THAT RUNS THROUGH THE FOREST BACK TO LIFE.

WHEN THAT HAPPENS, THE STUDENTS FROM MOUSEFORD ACADEMY TAKE A FIELD TRIP THROUGH THE FOREST, ENDING WITH A PICNIC IN A MEADOW, WHERE THEY WATCH THE DAM OPEN!

THE FIELD TRIP'S JUST A DAY AWAY, AND ALL THE STUDENTS ARE DOING THEIR BEST TO GET EVERYTHING READY!

YUM... SANDWICHES!

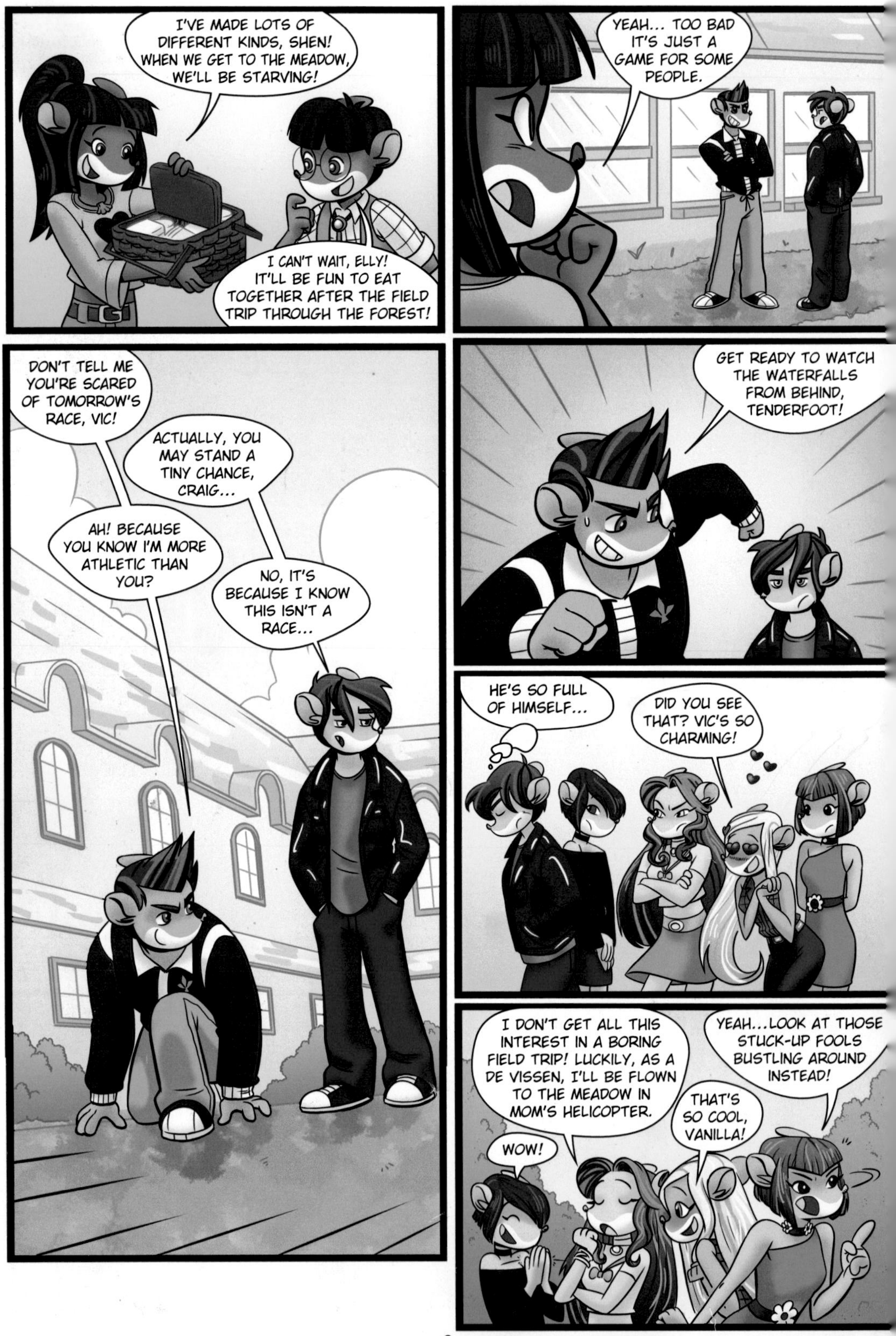
I'VE MADE LOTS OF DIFFERENT KINDS, SHEN! WHEN WE GET TO THE MEADOW, WE'LL BE STARVING!
I CAN'T WAIT, ELLY! IT'LL BE FUN TO EAT TOGETHER AFTER THE FIELD TRIP THROUGH THE FOREST!
YEAH... TOO BAD IT'S JUST A GAME FOR SOME PEOPLE.
DON'T TELL ME YOU'RE SCARED OF TOMORROW'S RACE, VIC!
ACTUALLY, YOU MAY STAND A TINY CHANCE, CRAIG...
AH! BECAUSE YOU KNOW I'M MORE ATHLETIC THAN YOU?
NO, IT'S BECAUSE I KNOW THIS ISN'T A RACE...
GET READY TO WATCH THE WATERFALLS FROM BEHIND, TENDERFOOT!
HE'S SO FULL OF HIMSELF...
DID YOU SEE THAT? VIC'S SO CHARMING!
I DON'T GET ALL THIS INTEREST IN A BORING FIELD TRIP! LUCKILY, AS A DE VISSEN, I'LL BE FLOWN TO THE MEADOW IN MOM'S HELICOPTER.
WOW!
THAT'S SO COOL, VANILLA!
YEAH...LOOK AT THOSE STUCK-UP FOOLS BUSTLING AROUND INSTEAD!

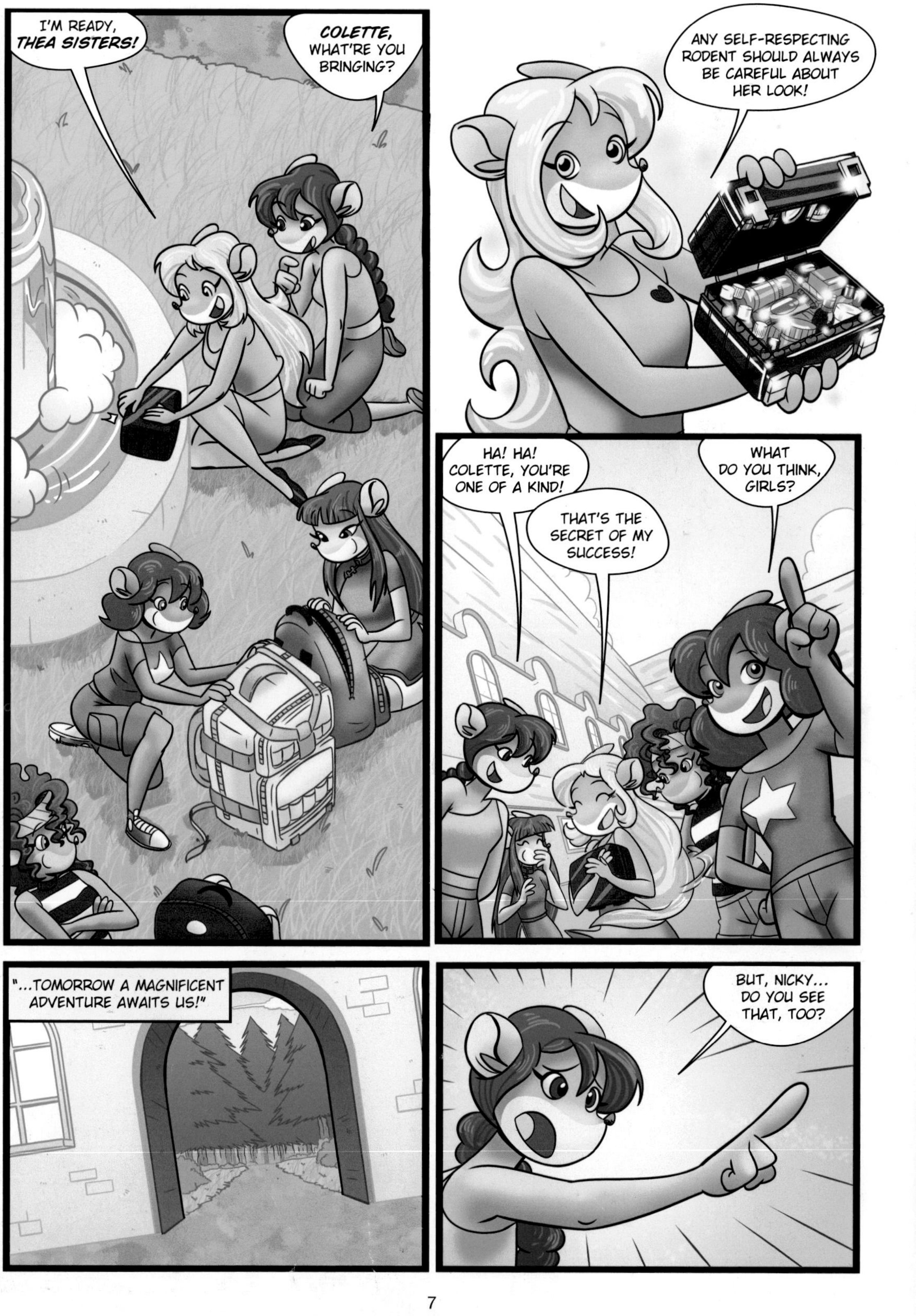
I'M READY, THEA SISTERS!
COLETTE, WHAT'RE YOU BRINGING?
ANY SELF-RESPECTING RODENT SHOULD ALWAYS BE CAREFUL ABOUT HER LOOK!
HA! HA! COLETTE, YOU'RE ONE OF A KIND!
THAT'S THE SECRET OF MY SUCCESS!
WHAT DO YOU THINK, GIRLS?
"...TOMORROW A MAGNIFICENT ADVENTURE AWAITS US!"
BUT, NICKY... DO YOU SEE THAT, TOO?

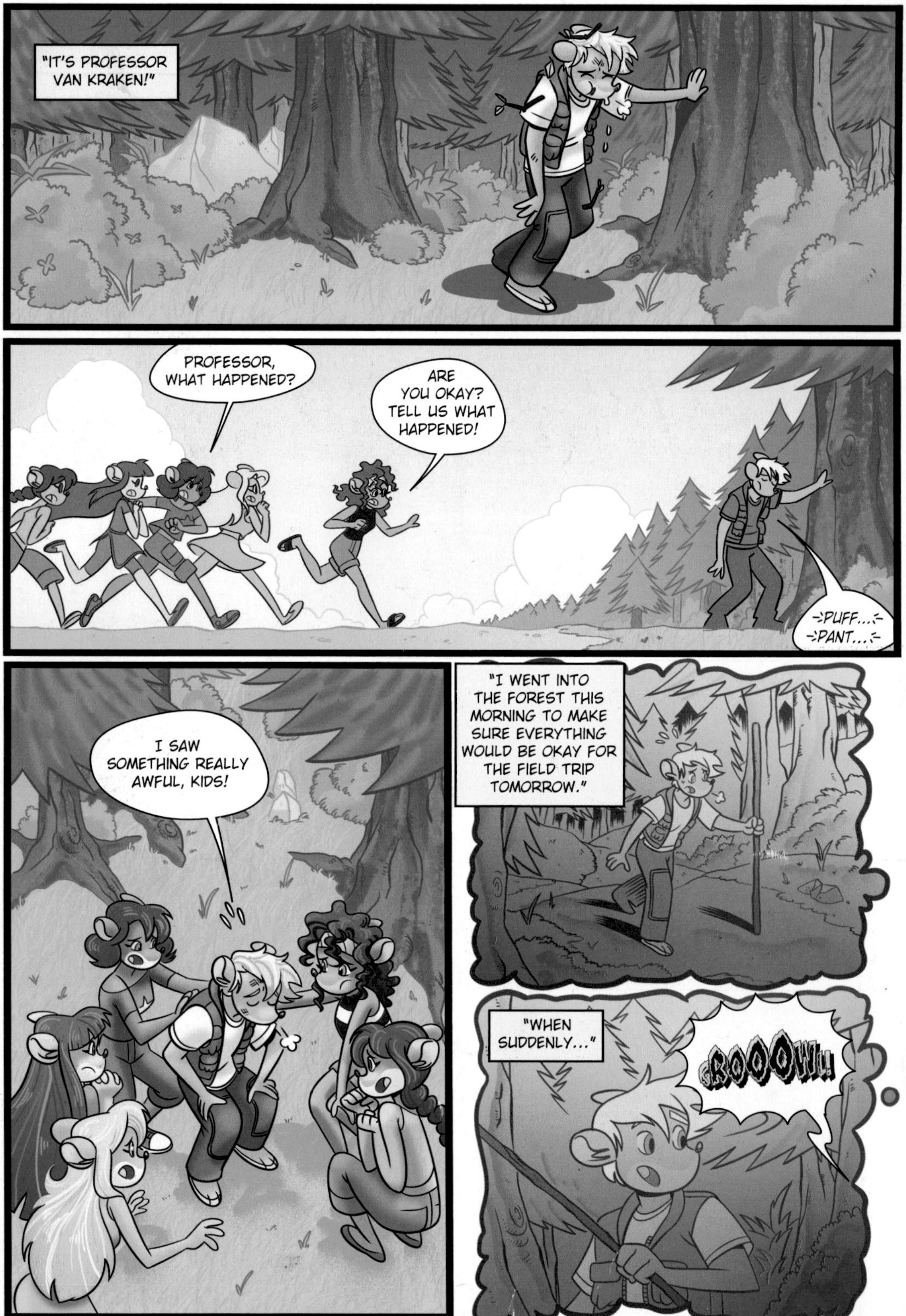
"IT'S PROFESSOR VAN KRAKEN!"
PROFESSOR, WHAT HAPPENED?
ARE YOU OKAY? TELL US WHAT HAPPENED!
PUFF... PANT...
I SAW SOMETHING REALLY AWFUL, KIDS!
"I WENT INTO THE FOREST THIS MORNING TO MAKE SURE EVERYTHING WOULD BE OKAY FOR THE FIELD TRIP TOMORROW."
"WHEN SUDDENLY..."
GROOOWL!

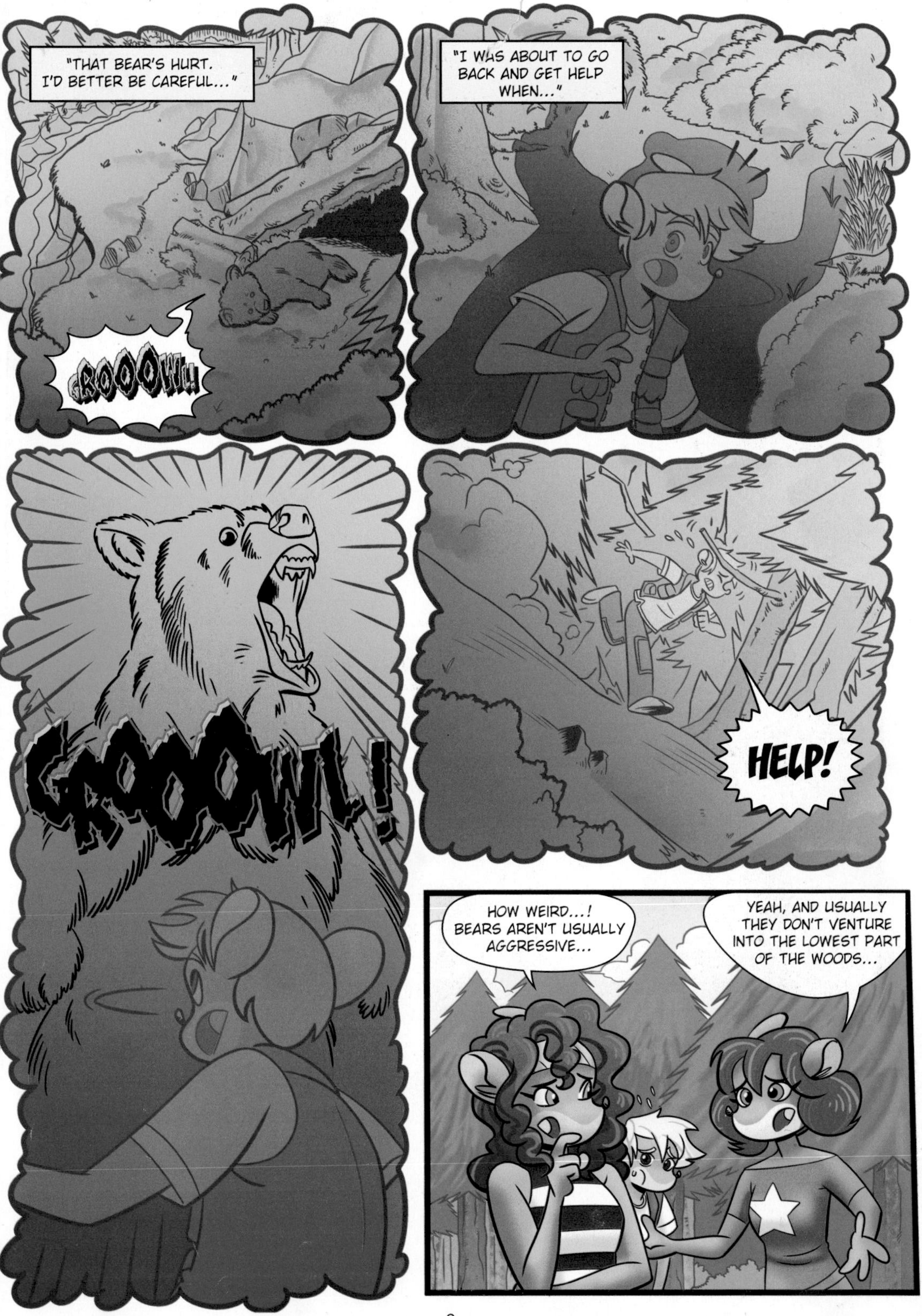
"THAT BEAR'S HURT. I'D BETTER BE CAREFUL..."
GROOOWL!!
"I WAS ABOUT TO GO BACK AND GET HELP WHEN..."
GROOOWL!
HELP!
HOW WEIRD...! BEARS AREN'T USUALLY AGGRESSIVE...
YEAH, AND USUALLY THEY DON'T VENTURE INTO THE LOWEST PART OF THE WOODS...

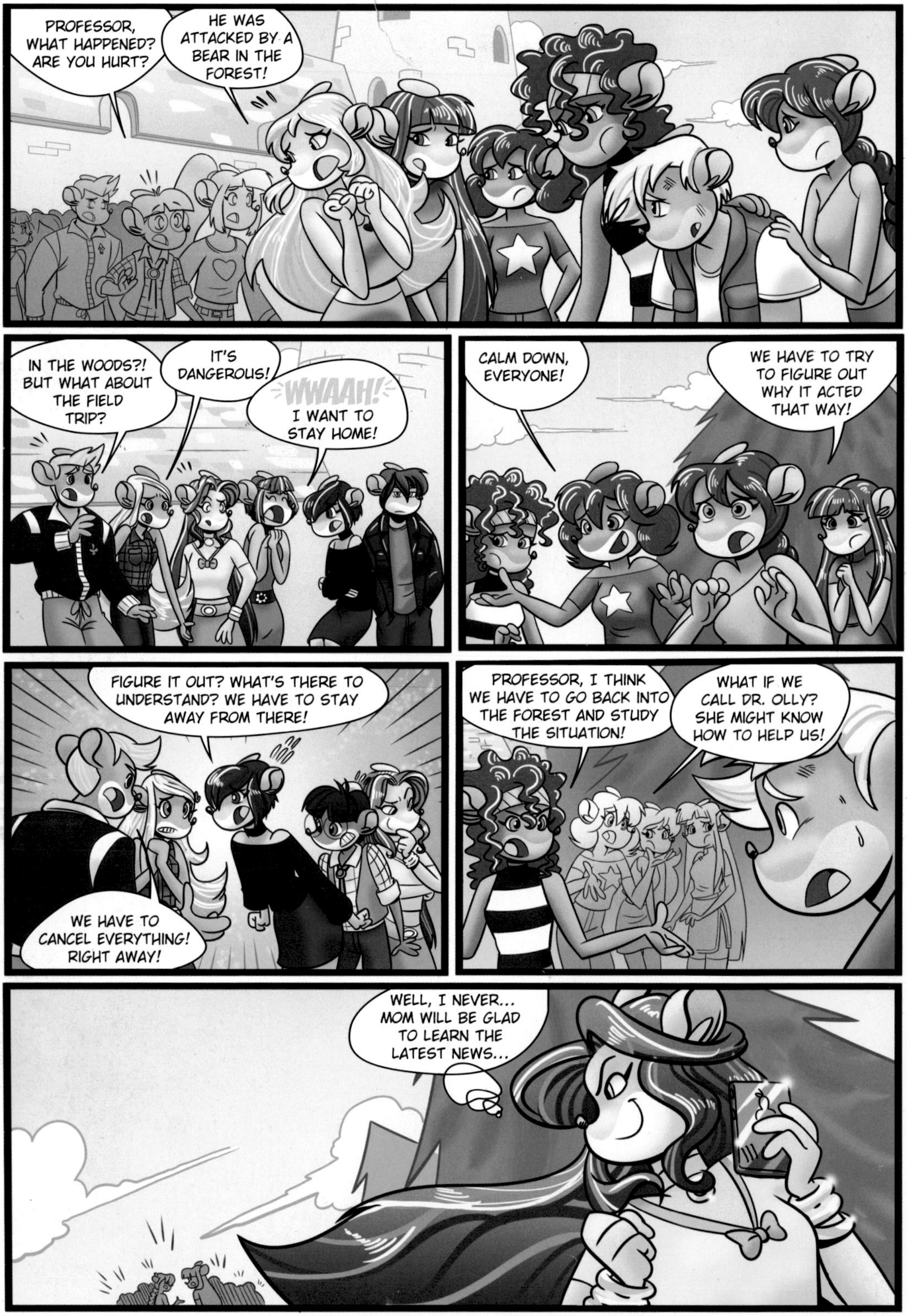
PROFESSOR, WHAT HAPPENED? ARE YOU HURT?
HE WAS ATTACKED BY A BEAR IN THE FOREST!
IN THE WOODS?! BUT WHAT ABOUT THE FIELD TRIP?
IT'S DANGEROUS!
WWAAH! I WANT TO STAY HOME!
CALM DOWN, EVERYONE!
WE HAVE TO TRY TO FIGURE OUT WHY IT ACTED THAT WAY!
FIGURE IT OUT? WHAT'S THERE TO UNDERSTAND? WE HAVE TO STAY AWAY FROM THERE!
WE HAVE TO CANCEL EVERYTHING! RIGHT AWAY!
PROFESSOR, I THINK WE HAVE TO GO BACK INTO THE FOREST AND STUDY THE SITUATION!
WHAT IF WE CALL DR. OLLY? SHE MIGHT KNOW HOW TO HELP US!
WELL, I NEVER... MOM WILL BE GLAD TO LEARN THE LATEST NEWS...

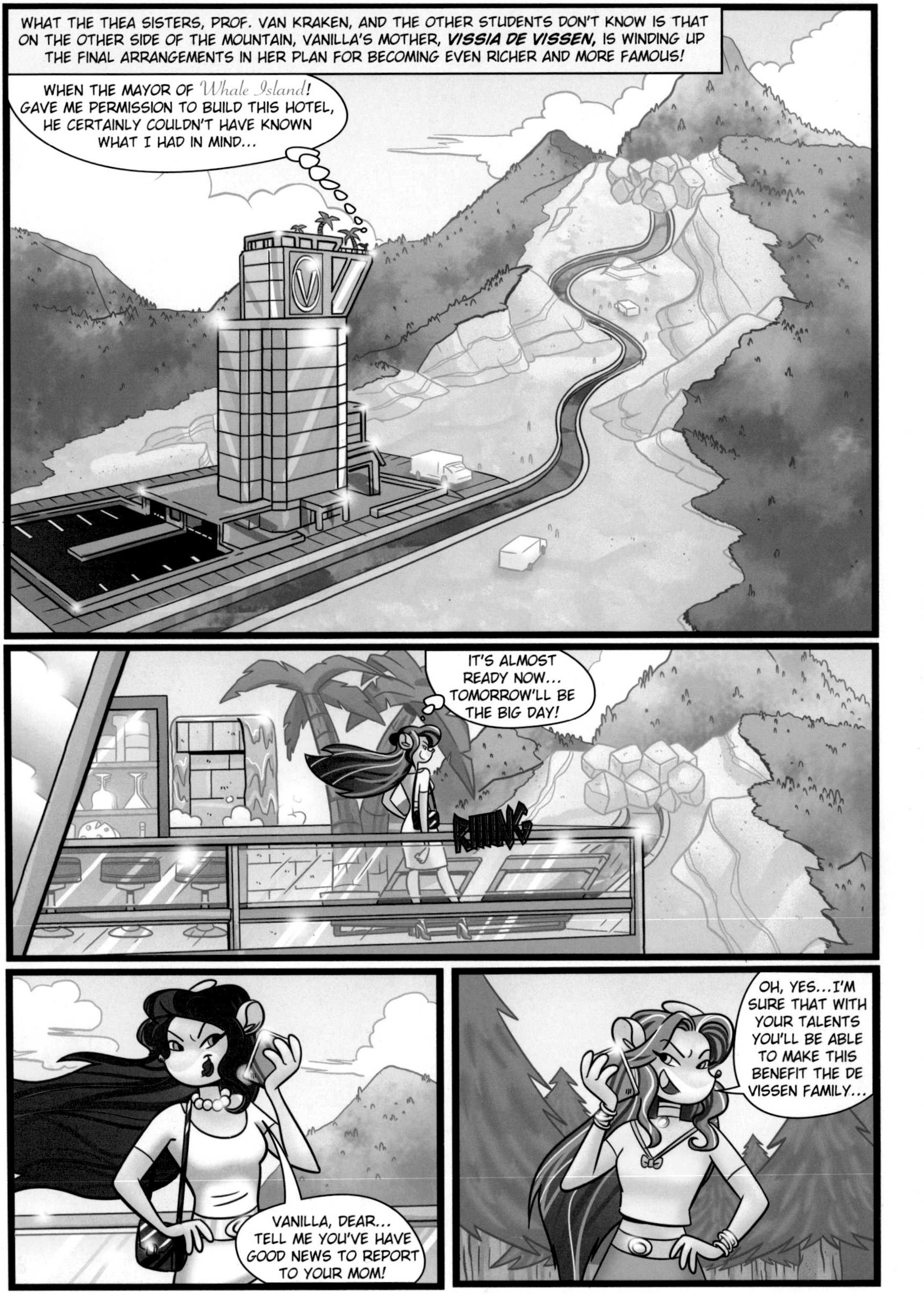
WHAT THE THEA SISTERS, PROF. VAN KRAKEN, AND THE OTHER STUDENTS DON'T KNOW IS THAT ON THE OTHER SIDE OF THE MOUNTAIN, VANILLA'S MOTHER, ***VISSIA DE VISSEN,*** IS WINDING UP THE FINAL ARRANGEMENTS IN HER PLAN FOR BECOMING EVEN RICHER AND MORE FAMOUS!
WHEN THE MAYOR OF *Whale Island*! GAVE ME PERMISSION TO BUILD THIS HOTEL, HE CERTAINLY COULDN'T HAVE KNOWN WHAT I HAD IN MIND...
IT'S ALMOST READY NOW... TOMORROW'LL BE THE BIG DAY!
RIIIING
VANILLA, DEAR... TELL ME YOU'VE HAVE GOOD NEWS TO REPORT TO YOUR MOM!
OH, YES...I'M SURE THAT WITH YOUR TALENTS YOU'LL BE ABLE TO MAKE THIS BENEFIT THE DE VISSEN FAMILY...

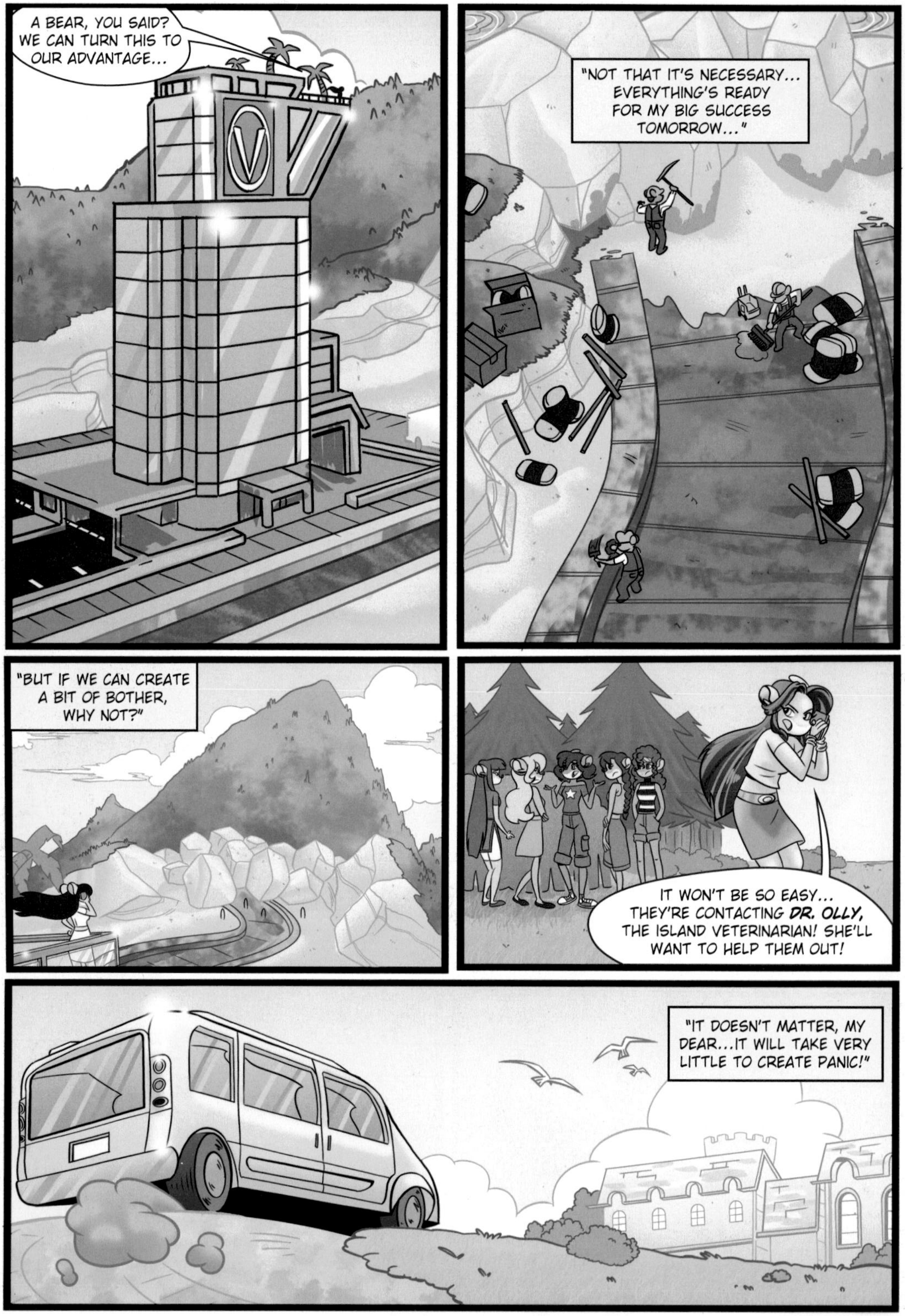
A BEAR, YOU SAID? WE CAN TURN THIS TO OUR ADVANTAGE...
"NOT THAT IT'S NECESSARY... EVERYTHING'S READY FOR MY BIG SUCCESS TOMORROW..."
"BUT IF WE CAN CREATE A BIT OF BOTHER, WHY NOT?"
IT WON'T BE SO EASY... THEY'RE CONTACTING DR. OLLY, THE ISLAND VETERINARIAN! SHE'LL WANT TO HELP THEM OUT!
"IT DOESN'T MATTER, MY DEAR...IT WILL TAKE VERY LITTLE TO CREATE PANIC!"

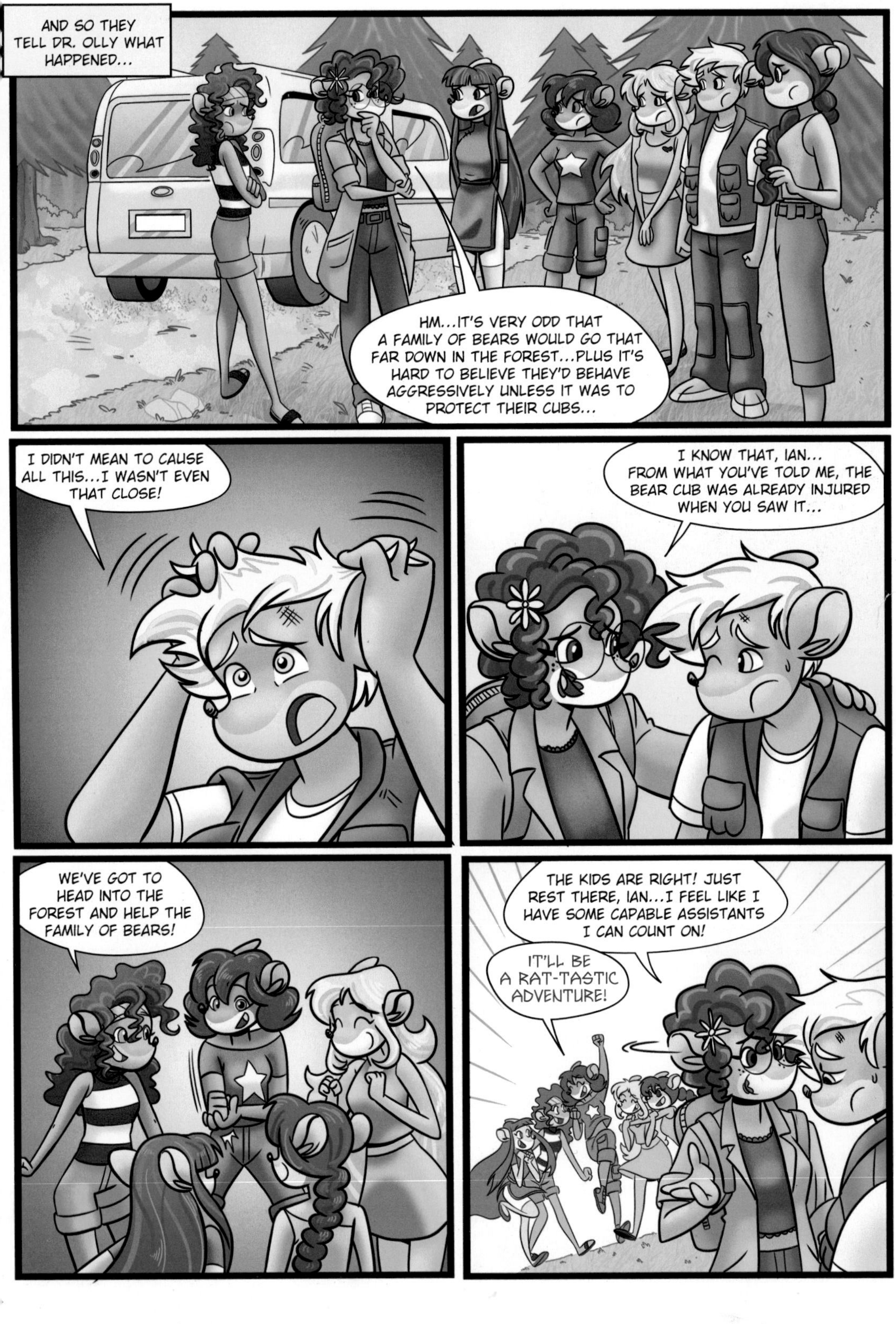
AND SO THEY TELL DR. OLLY WHAT HAPPENED...
HM...IT'S VERY ODD THAT A FAMILY OF BEARS WOULD GO THAT FAR DOWN IN THE FOREST...PLUS IT'S HARD TO BELIEVE THEY'D BEHAVE AGGRESSIVELY UNLESS IT WAS TO PROTECT THEIR CUBS...
I DIDN'T MEAN TO CAUSE ALL THIS...I WASN'T EVEN THAT CLOSE!
I KNOW THAT, IAN... FROM WHAT YOU'VE TOLD ME, THE BEAR CUB WAS ALREADY INJURED WHEN YOU SAW IT...
WE'VE GOT TO HEAD INTO THE FOREST AND HELP THE FAMILY OF BEARS!
THE KIDS ARE RIGHT! JUST REST THERE, IAN...I FEEL LIKE I HAVE SOME CAPABLE ASSISTANTS I CAN COUNT ON!
IT'LL BE A RAT-TASTIC ADVENTURE!

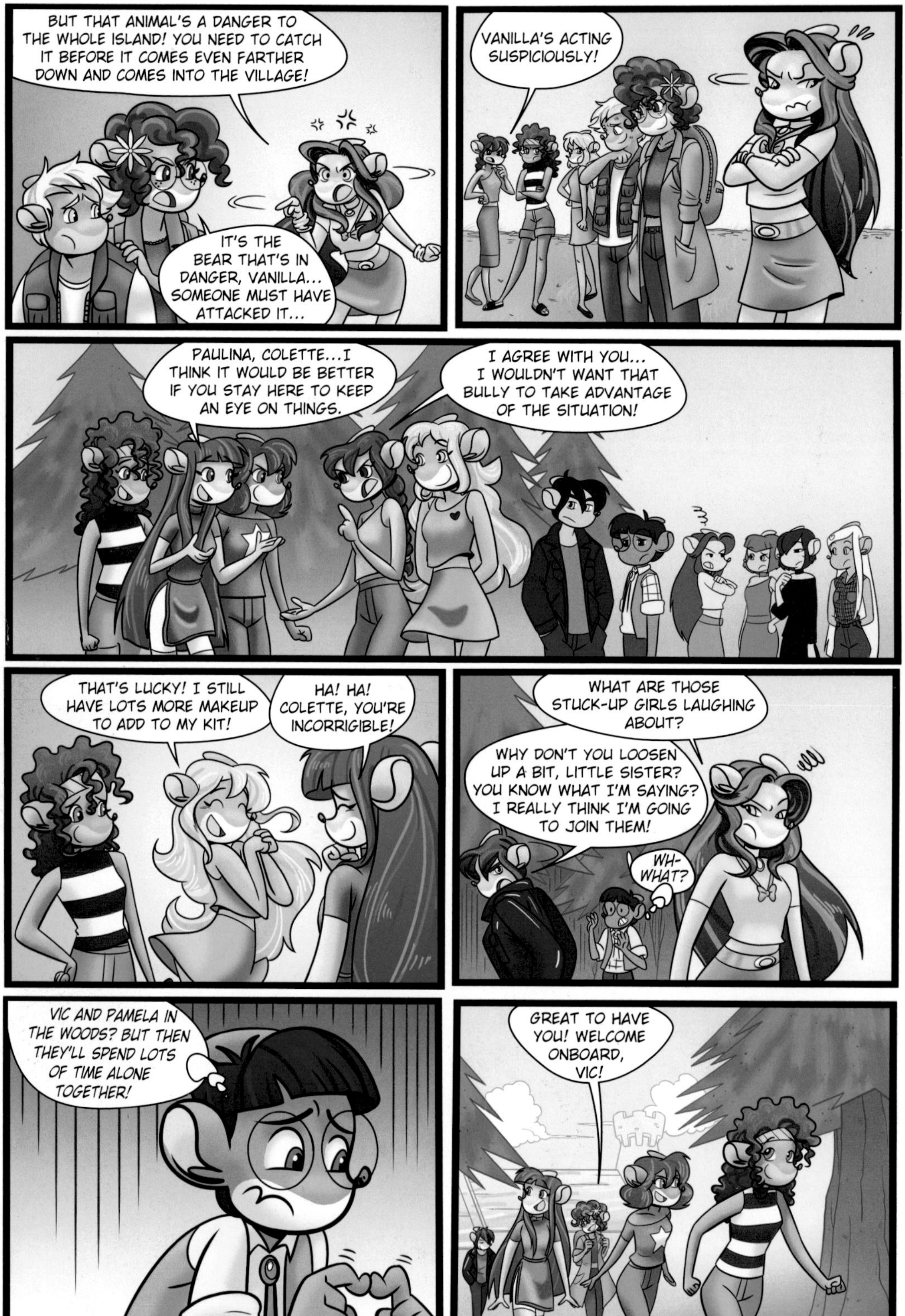
BUT THAT ANIMAL'S A DANGER TO THE WHOLE ISLAND! YOU NEED TO CATCH IT BEFORE IT COMES EVEN FARTHER DOWN AND COMES INTO THE VILLAGE!
IT'S THE BEAR THAT'S IN DANGER, VANILLA... SOMEONE MUST HAVE ATTACKED IT...
VANILLA'S ACTING SUSPICIOUSLY!
PAULINA, COLETTE...I THINK IT WOULD BE BETTER IF YOU STAY HERE TO KEEP AN EYE ON THINGS.
I AGREE WITH YOU... I WOULDN'T WANT THAT BULLY TO TAKE ADVANTAGE OF THE SITUATION!
THAT'S LUCKY! I STILL HAVE LOTS MORE MAKEUP TO ADD TO MY KIT!
HA! HA! COLETTE, YOU'RE INCORRIGIBLE!
WHAT ARE THOSE STUCK-UP GIRLS LAUGHING ABOUT?
WHY DON'T YOU LOOSEN UP A BIT, LITTLE SISTER? YOU KNOW WHAT I'M SAYING? I REALLY THINK I'M GOING TO JOIN THEM!
WH-WHAT?
VIC AND PAMELA IN THE WOODS? BUT THEN THEY'LL SPEND LOTS OF TIME ALONE TOGETHER!
GREAT TO HAVE YOU! WELCOME ONBOARD, VIC!

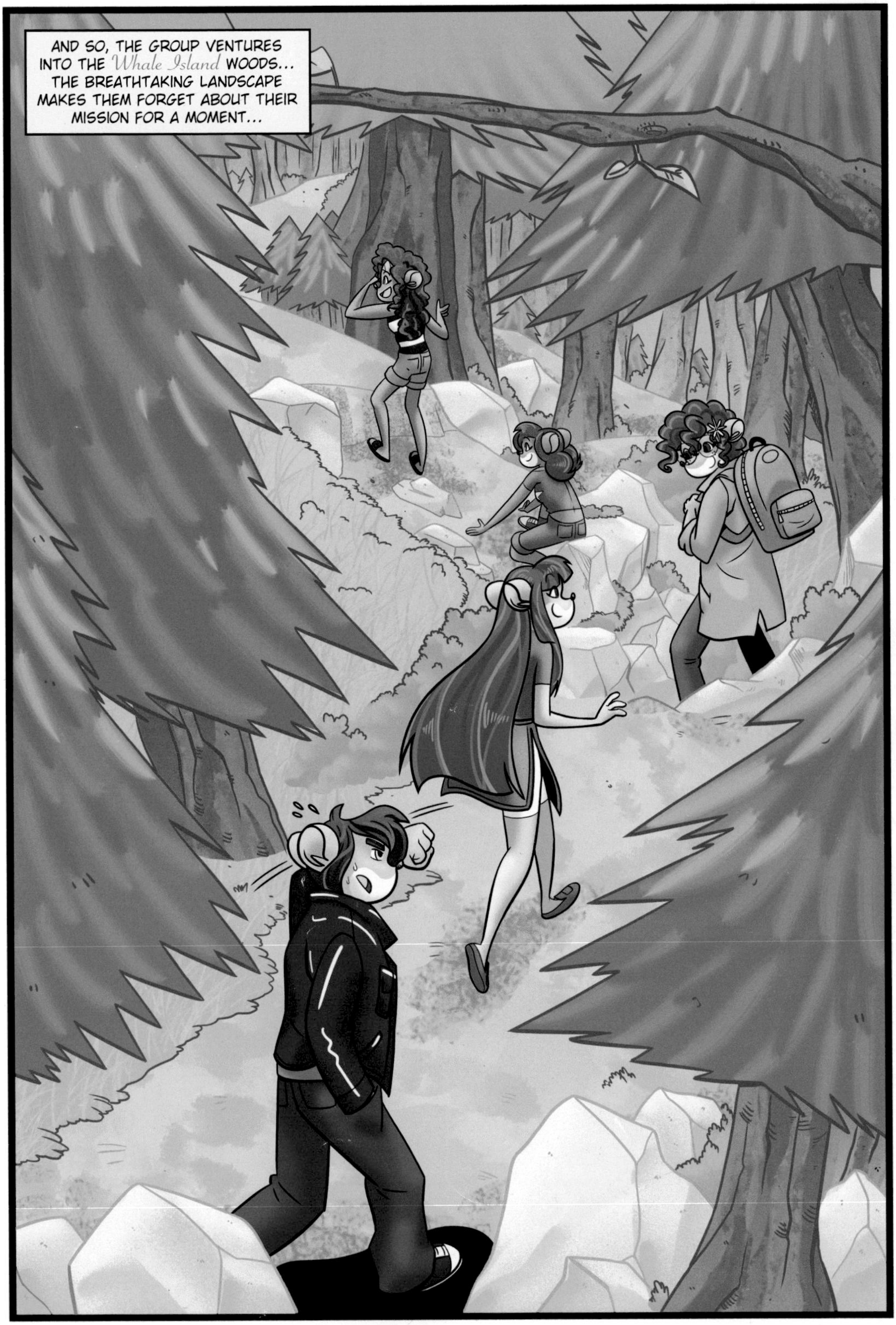
AND SO, THE GROUP VENTURES INTO THE *Whale Island* WOODS... THE BREATHTAKING LANDSCAPE MAKES THEM FORGET ABOUT THEIR MISSION FOR A MOMENT...

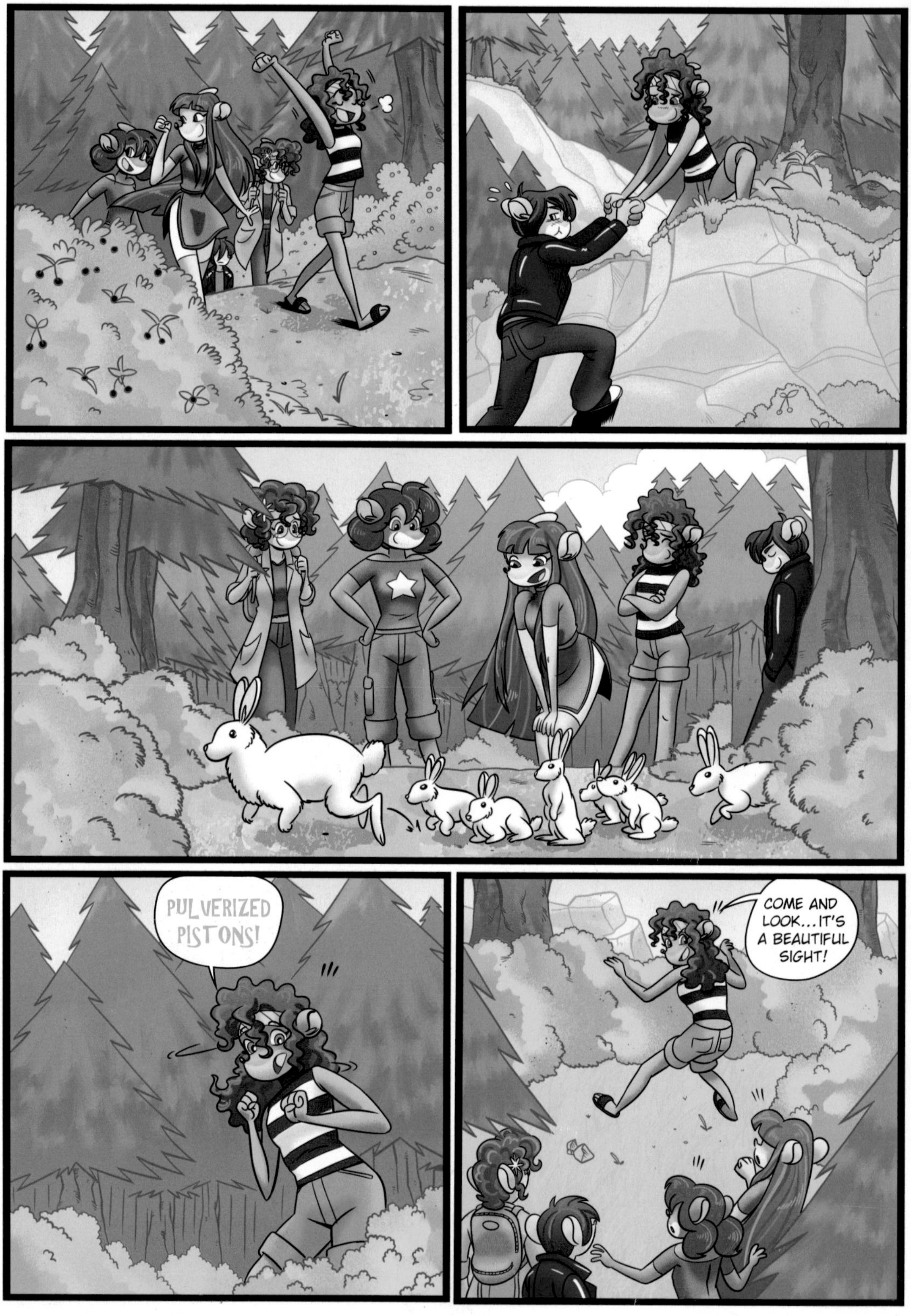
PULVERIZED PISTONS!
COME AND LOOK... IT'S A BEAUTIFUL SIGHT!

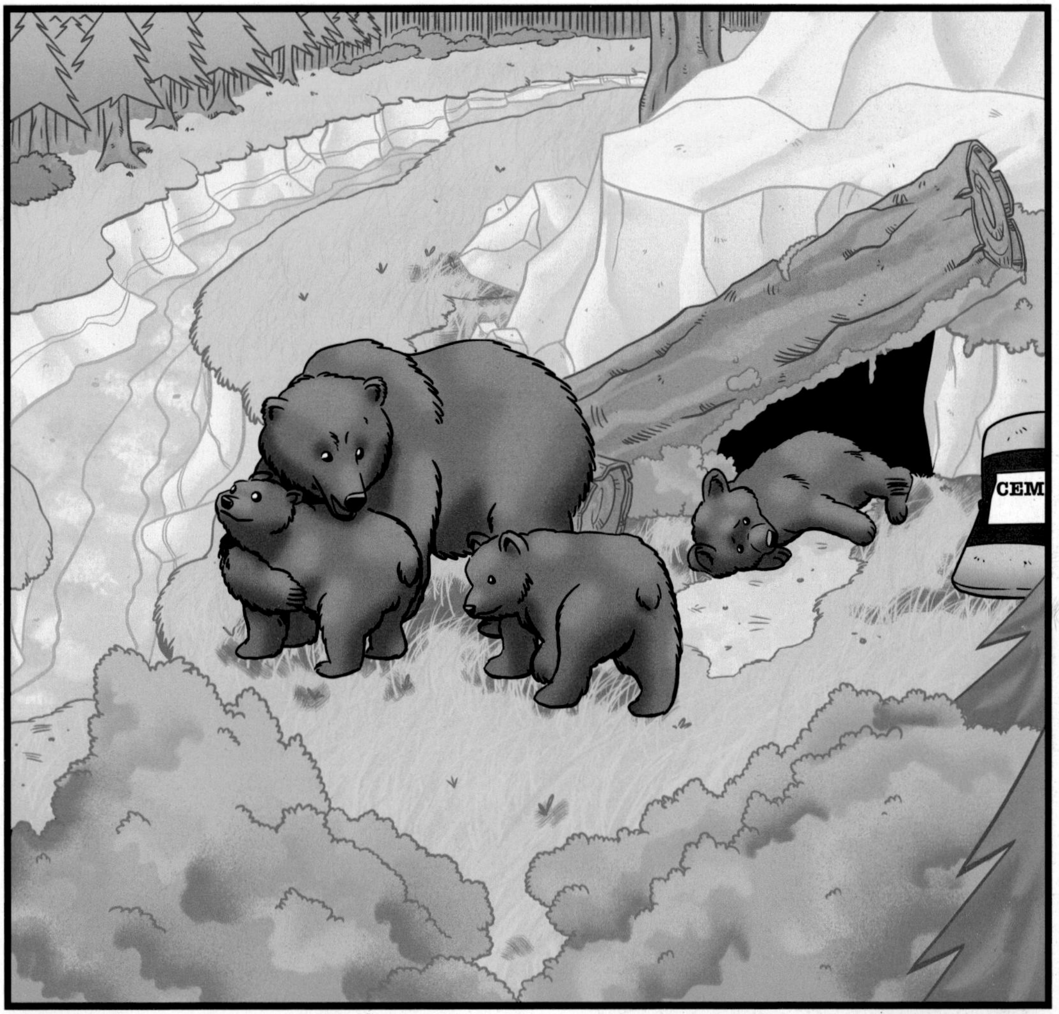
CEM

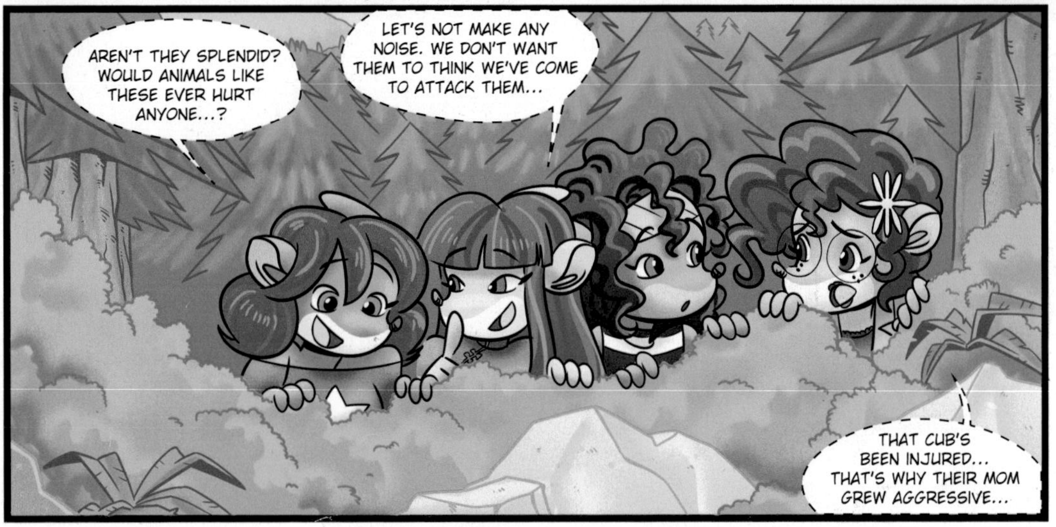
AREN'T THEY SPLENDID? WOULD ANIMALS LIKE THESE EVER HURT ANYONE...?
LET'S NOT MAKE ANY NOISE. WE DON'T WANT THEM TO THINK WE'VE COME TO ATTACK THEM...
THAT CUB'S BEEN INJURED... THAT'S WHY THEIR MOM GREW AGGRESSIVE...

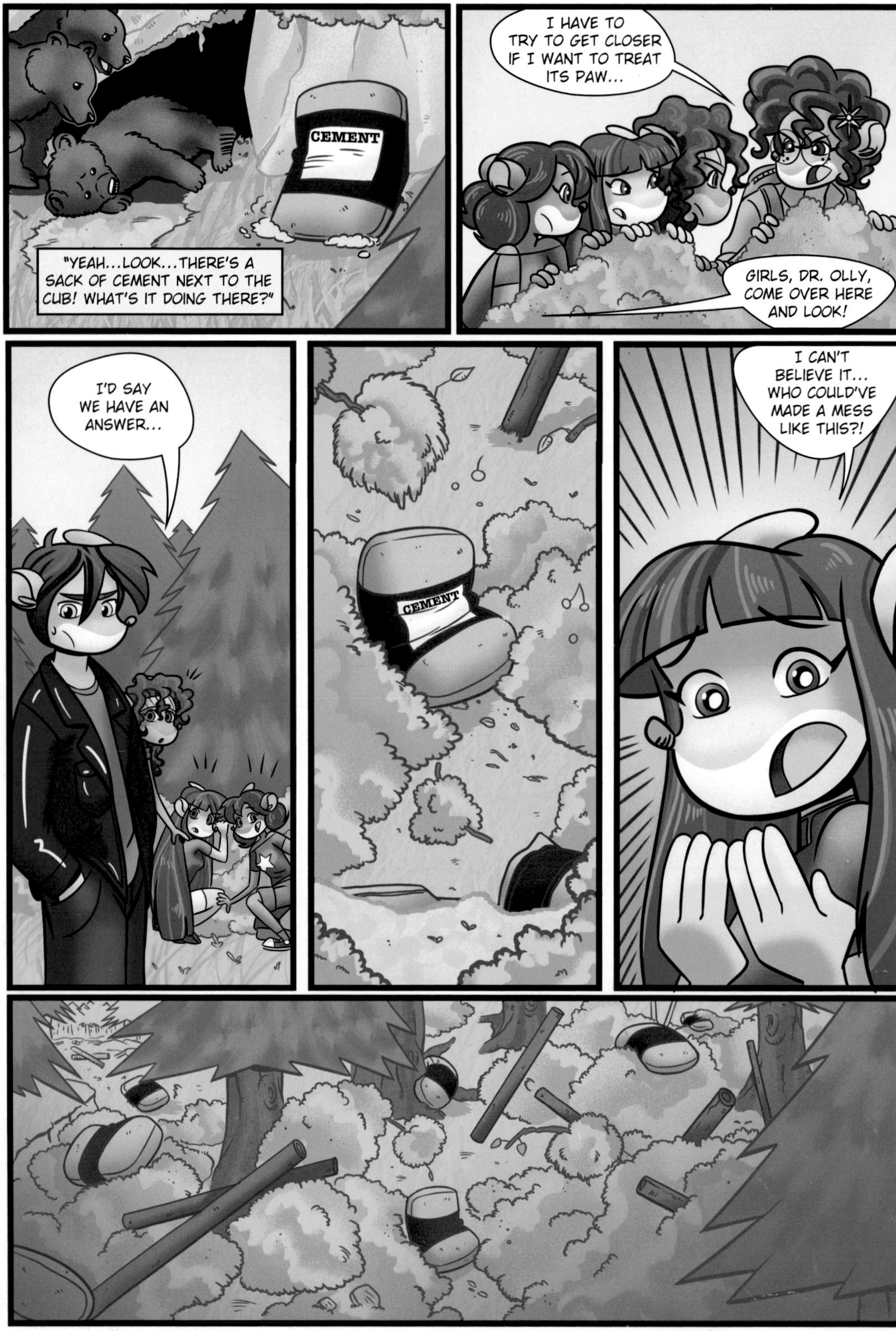
CEMENT
"YEAH...LOOK...THERE'S A SACK OF CEMENT NEXT TO THE CUB! WHAT'S IT DOING THERE?"
I HAVE TO TRY TO GET CLOSER IF I WANT TO TREAT ITS PAW...
GIRLS, DR. OLLY, COME OVER HERE AND LOOK!
I'D SAY WE HAVE AN ANSWER...
CEMENT
I CAN'T BELIEVE IT... WHO COULD'VE MADE A MESS LIKE THIS?!

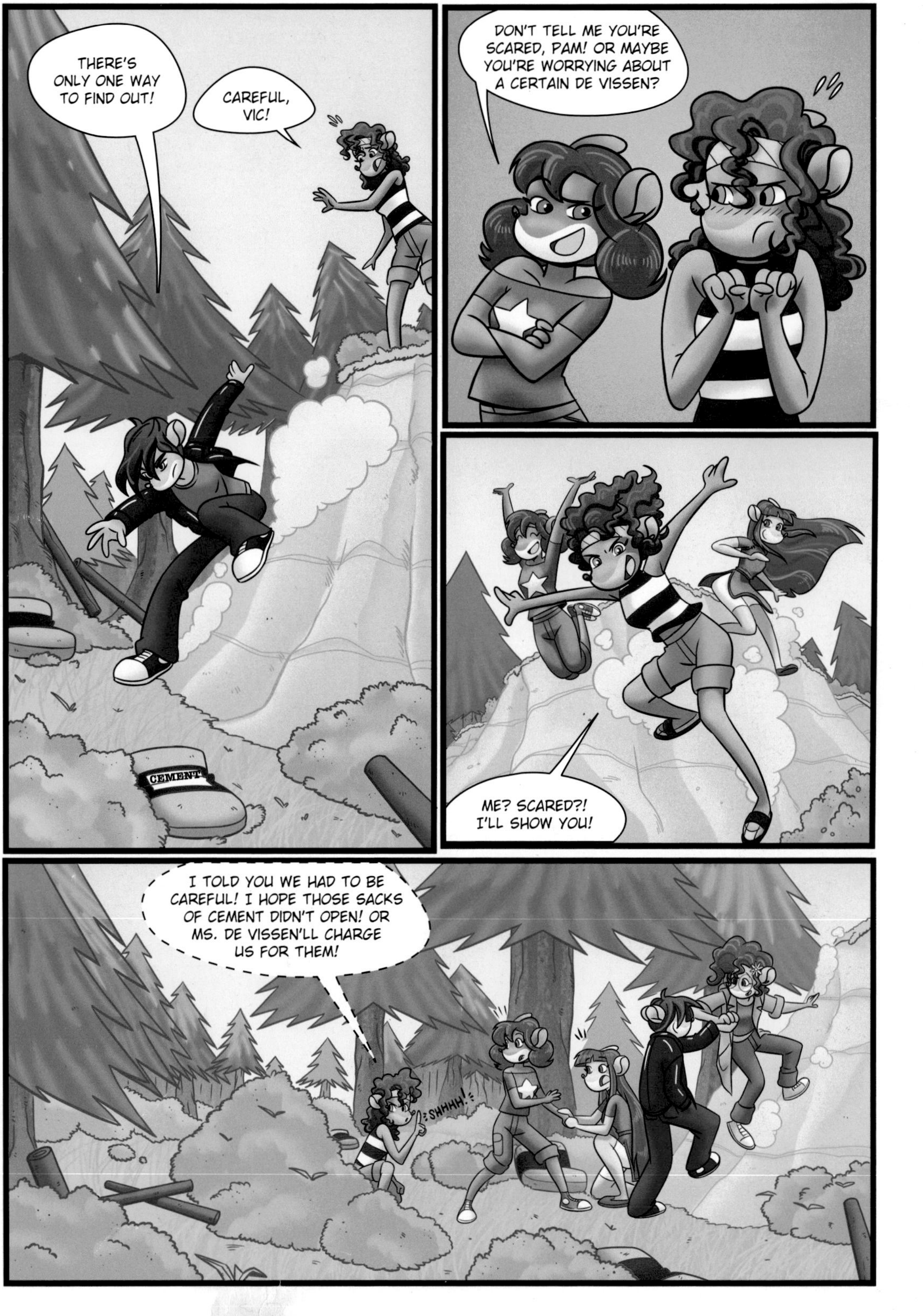
THERE'S ONLY ONE WAY TO FIND OUT!
CAREFUL, VIC!
DON'T TELL ME YOU'RE SCARED, PAM! OR MAYBE YOU'RE WORRYING ABOUT A CERTAIN DE VISSEN?
ME? SCARED?! I'LL SHOW YOU!
CEMENT
I TOLD YOU WE HAD TO BE CAREFUL! I HOPE THOSE SACKS OF CEMENT DIDN'T OPEN! OR MS. DE VISSEN'LL CHARGE US FOR THEM!
SHHHH!

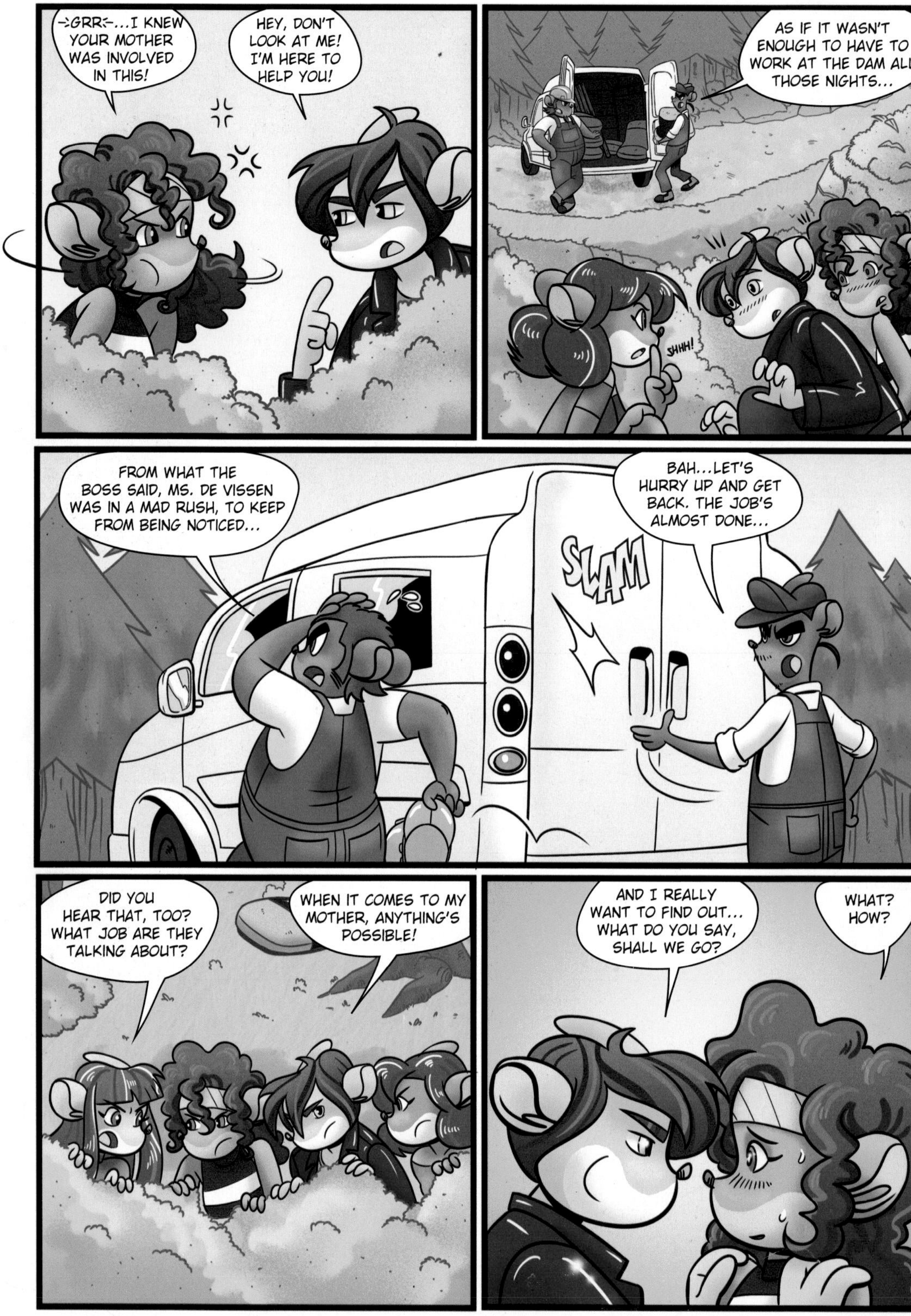

-GRR-...I KNEW YOUR MOTHER WAS INVOLVED IN THIS!
HEY, DON'T LOOK AT ME! I'M HERE TO HELP YOU!
AS IF IT WASN'T ENOUGH TO HAVE TO WORK AT THE DAM ALL THOSE NIGHTS...
SHHH!
FROM WHAT THE BOSS SAID, MS. DE VISSEN WAS IN A MAD RUSH, TO KEEP FROM BEING NOTICED...
BAH...LET'S HURRY UP AND GET BACK. THE JOB'S ALMOST DONE...
SLAM
DID YOU HEAR THAT, TOO? WHAT JOB ARE THEY TALKING ABOUT?
WHEN IT COMES TO MY MOTHER, ANYTHING'S POSSIBLE!
AND I REALLY WANT TO FIND OUT... WHAT DO YOU SAY, SHALL WE GO?
WHAT? HOW?

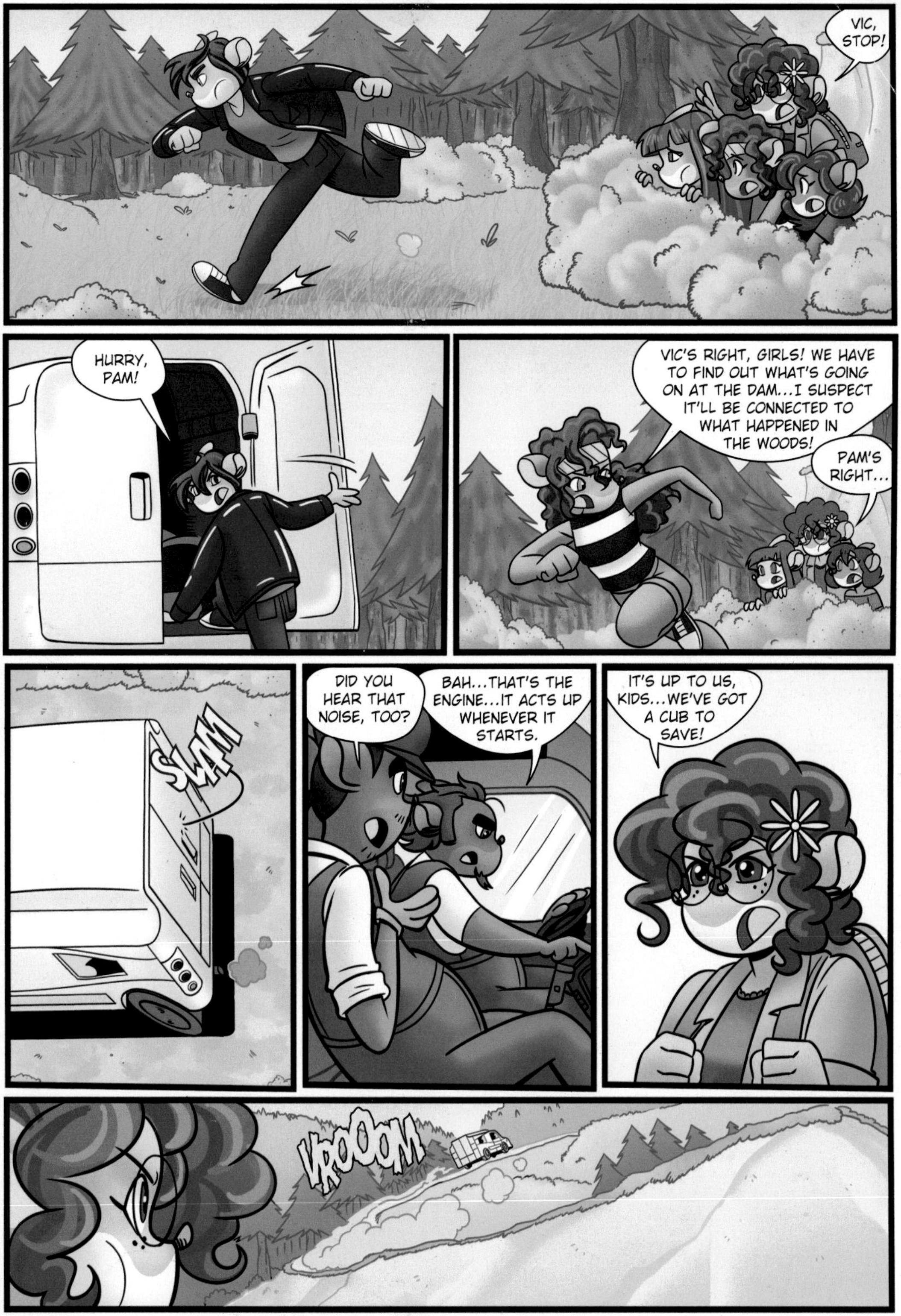
VIC, STOP!
HURRY, PAM!
VIC'S RIGHT, GIRLS! WE HAVE TO FIND OUT WHAT'S GOING ON AT THE DAM...I SUSPECT IT'LL BE CONNECTED TO WHAT HAPPENED IN THE WOODS!
PAM'S RIGHT...
SLAM
DID YOU HEAR THAT NOISE, TOO?
BAH...THAT'S THE ENGINE...IT ACTS UP WHENEVER IT STARTS.
IT'S UP TO US, KIDS...WE'VE GOT A CUB TO SAVE!
VROOOM

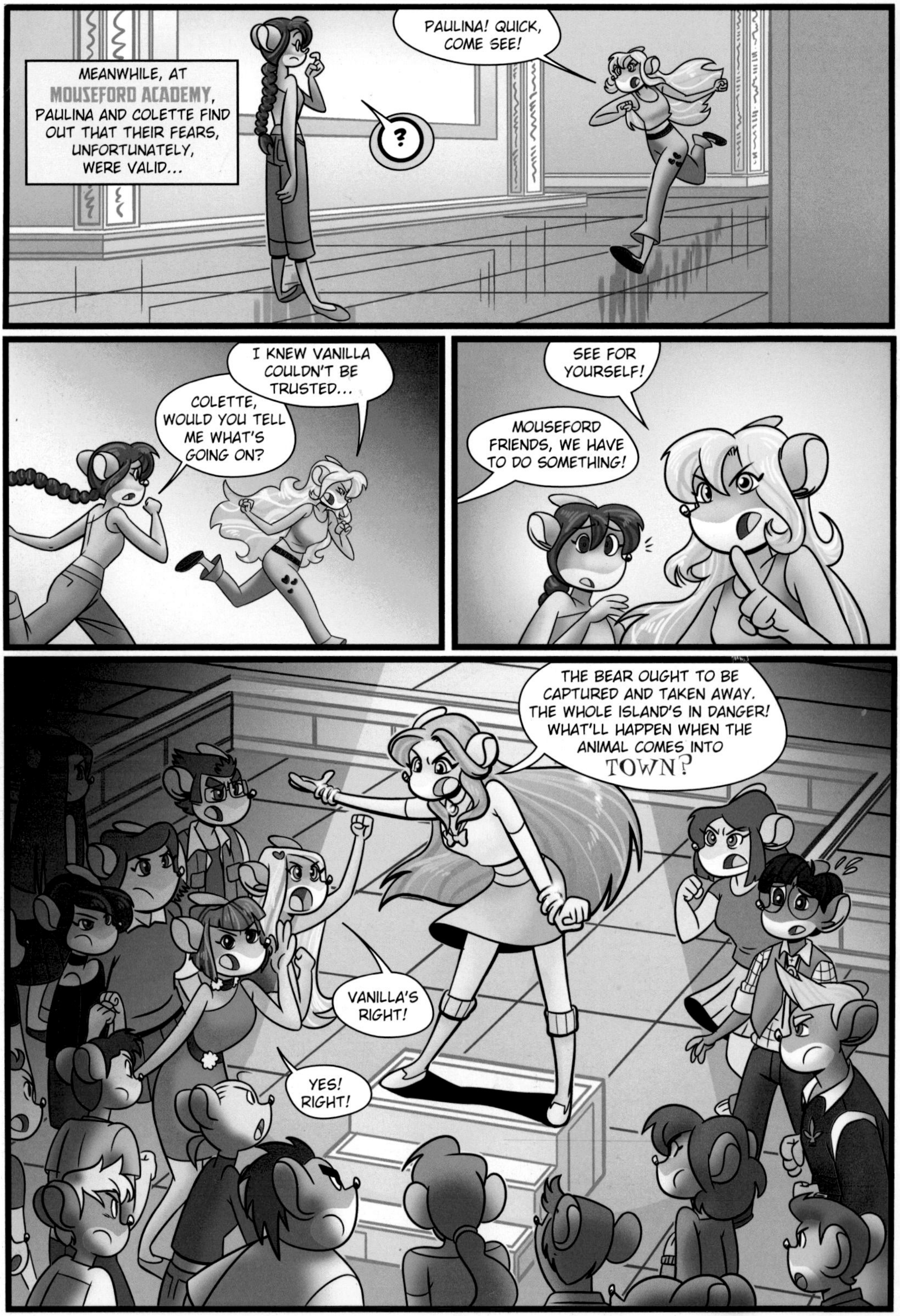
MEANWHILE, AT MOUSEFORD ACADEMY, PAULINA AND COLETTE FIND OUT THAT THEIR FEARS, UNFORTUNATELY, WERE VALID...
PAULINA! QUICK, COME SEE!
?
I KNEW VANILLA COULDN'T BE TRUSTED...
COLETTE, WOULD YOU TELL ME WHAT'S GOING ON?
SEE FOR YOURSELF!
MOUSEFORD FRIENDS, WE HAVE TO DO SOMETHING!
THE BEAR OUGHT TO BE CAPTURED AND TAKEN AWAY. THE WHOLE ISLAND'S IN DANGER! WHAT'LL HAPPEN WHEN THE ANIMAL COMES INTO TOWN?
VANILLA'S RIGHT!
YES! RIGHT!

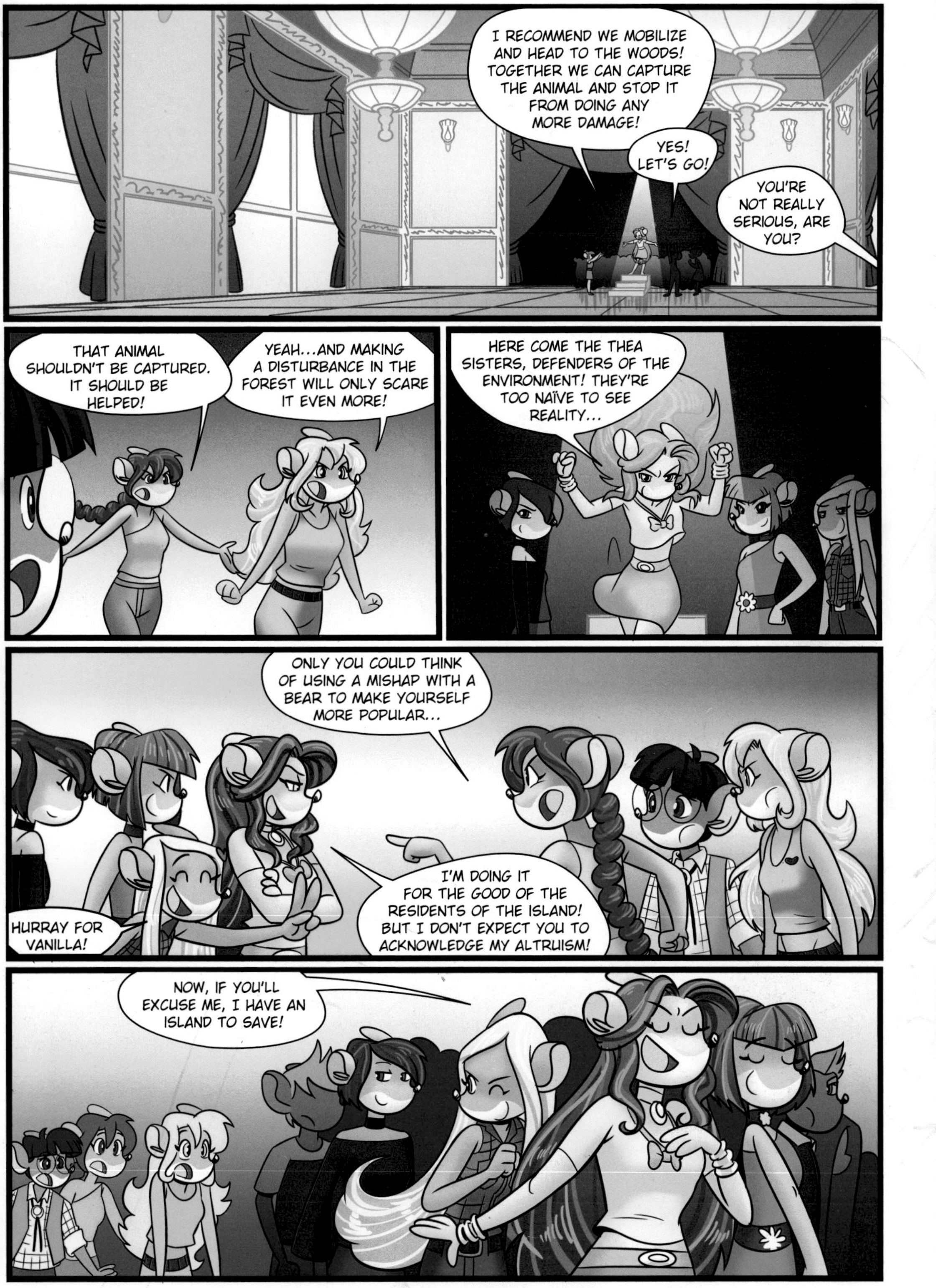
I RECOMMEND WE MOBILIZE AND HEAD TO THE WOODS! TOGETHER WE CAN CAPTURE THE ANIMAL AND STOP IT FROM DOING ANY MORE DAMAGE!
YES! LET'S GO!
YOU'RE NOT REALLY SERIOUS, ARE YOU?
THAT ANIMAL SHOULDN'T BE CAPTURED. IT SHOULD BE HELPED!
YEAH...AND MAKING A DISTURBANCE IN THE FOREST WILL ONLY SCARE IT EVEN MORE!
HERE COME THE THEA SISTERS, DEFENDERS OF THE ENVIRONMENT! THEY'RE TOO NAÏVE TO SEE REALITY...
ONLY YOU COULD THINK OF USING A MISHAP WITH A BEAR TO MAKE YOURSELF MORE POPULAR...
I'M DOING IT FOR THE GOOD OF THE RESIDENTS OF THE ISLAND! BUT I DON'T EXPECT YOU TO ACKNOWLEDGE MY ALTRUISM!
HURRAY FOR VANILLA!
NOW, IF YOU'LL EXCUSE ME, I HAVE AN ISLAND TO SAVE!

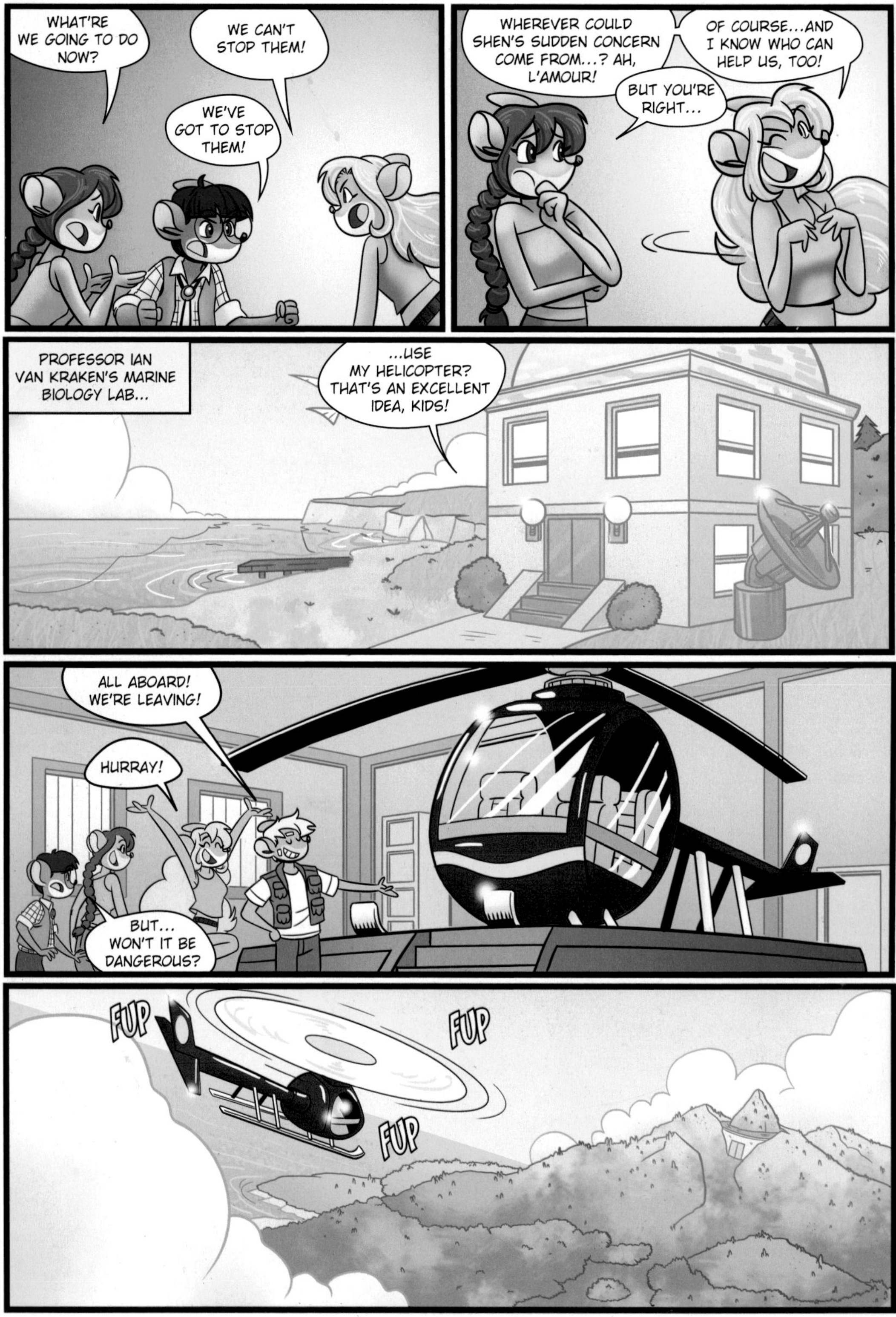

WHAT'RE WE GOING TO DO NOW?
WE CAN'T STOP THEM!
WE'VE GOT TO STOP THEM!
WHEREVER COULD SHEN'S SUDDEN CONCERN COME FROM...? AH, L'AMOUR!
BUT YOU'RE RIGHT...
OF COURSE...AND I KNOW WHO CAN HELP US, TOO!
PROFESSOR IAN VAN KRAKEN'S MARINE BIOLOGY LAB...
...USE MY HELICOPTER? THAT'S AN EXCELLENT IDEA, KIDS!
ALL ABOARD! WE'RE LEAVING!
HURRAY!
BUT... WON'T IT BE DANGEROUS?
FUP
FUP
FUP

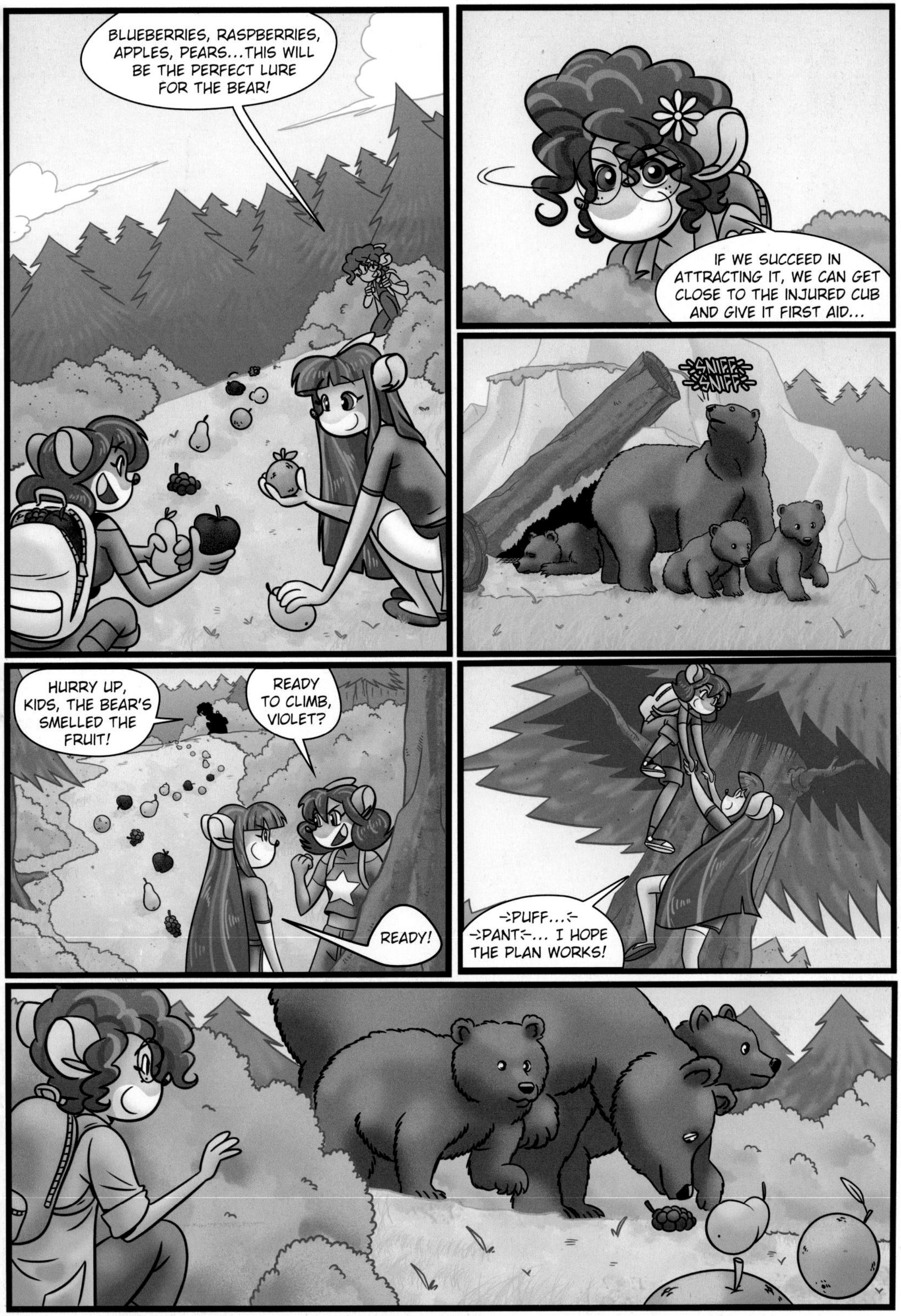
BLUEBERRIES, RASPBERRIES, APPLES, PEARS...THIS WILL BE THE PERFECT LURE FOR THE BEAR!
IF WE SUCCEED IN ATTRACTING IT, WE CAN GET CLOSE TO THE INJURED CUB AND GIVE IT FIRST AID...
SNIFF SNIFF
HURRY UP, KIDS, THE BEAR'S SMELLED THE FRUIT!
READY TO CLIMB, VIOLET?
READY!
PUFF... PANT... I HOPE THE PLAN WORKS!

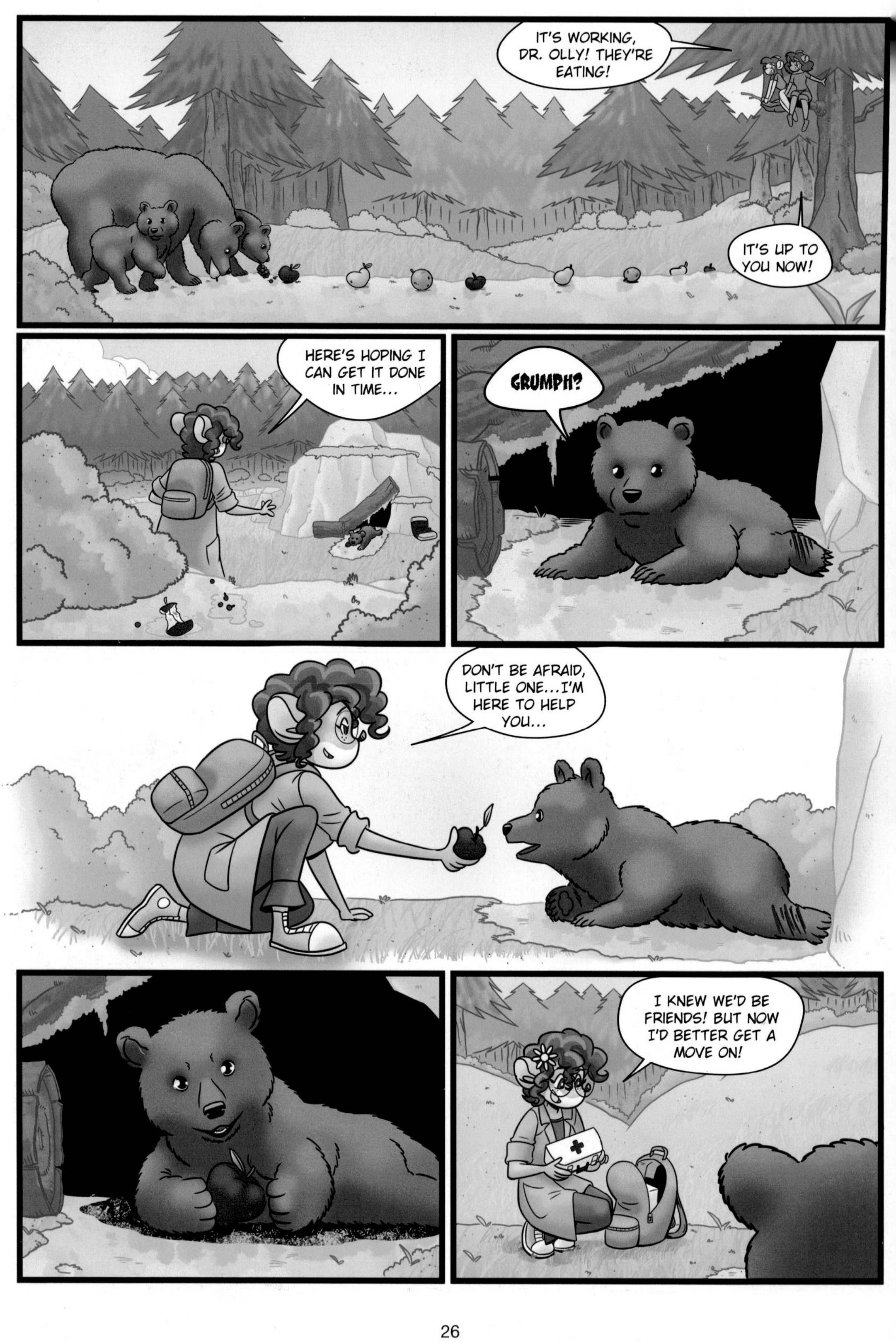
IT'S WORKING, DR. OLLY! THEY'RE EATING!
IT'S UP TO YOU NOW!
HERE'S HOPING I CAN GET IT DONE IN TIME...
GRUMPH?
DON'T BE AFRAID, LITTLE ONE...I'M HERE TO HELP YOU...
I KNEW WE'D BE FRIENDS! BUT NOW I'D BETTER GET A MOVE ON!

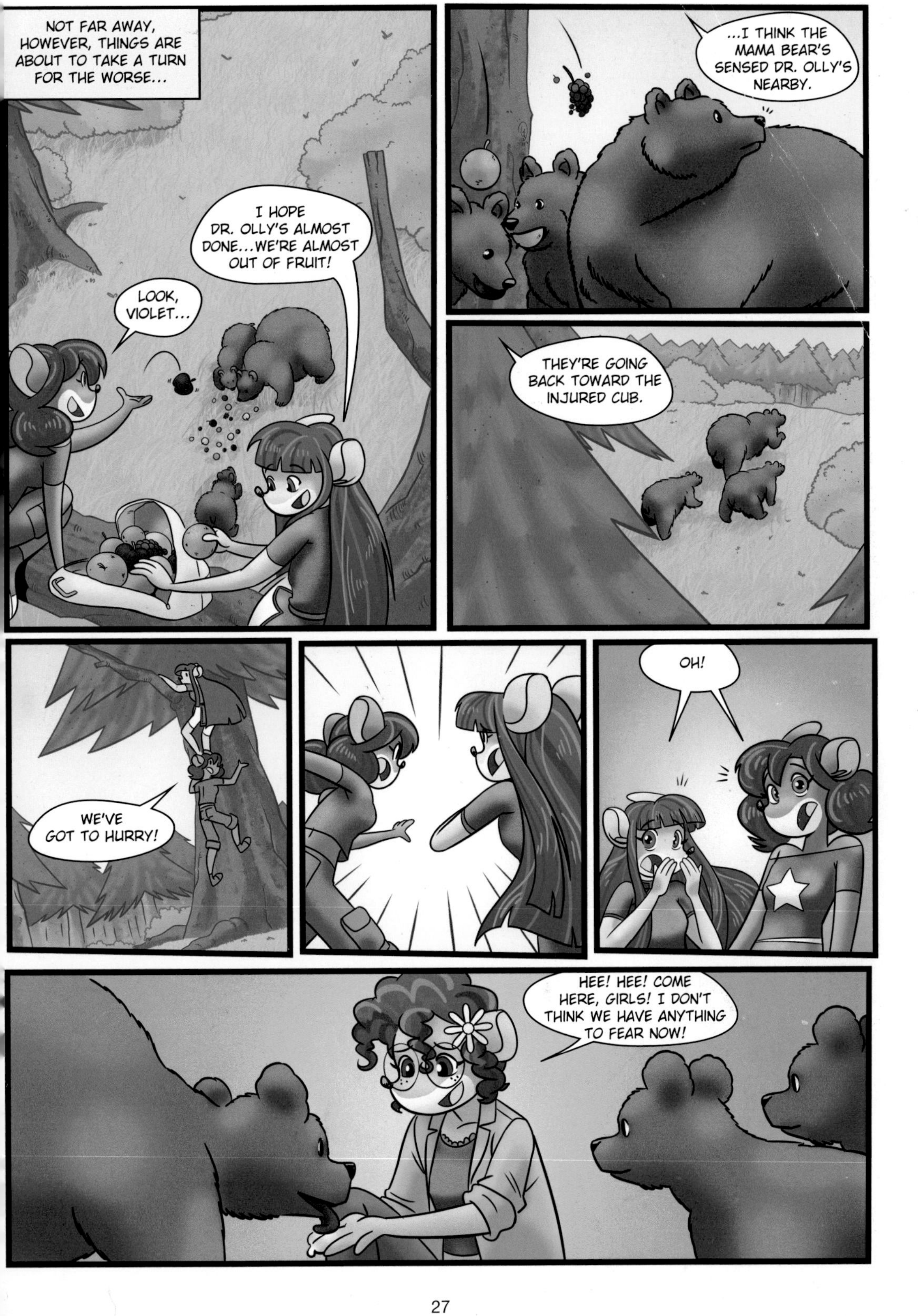
NOT FAR AWAY, HOWEVER, THINGS ARE ABOUT TO TAKE A TURN FOR THE WORSE...
I HOPE DR. OLLY'S ALMOST DONE...WE'RE ALMOST OUT OF FRUIT!
LOOK, VIOLET...
...I THINK THE MAMA BEAR'S SENSED DR. OLLY'S NEARBY.
THEY'RE GOING BACK TOWARD THE INJURED CUB.
WE'VE GOT TO HURRY!
OH!
HEE! HEE! COME HERE, GIRLS! I DON'T THINK WE HAVE ANYTHING TO FEAR NOW!

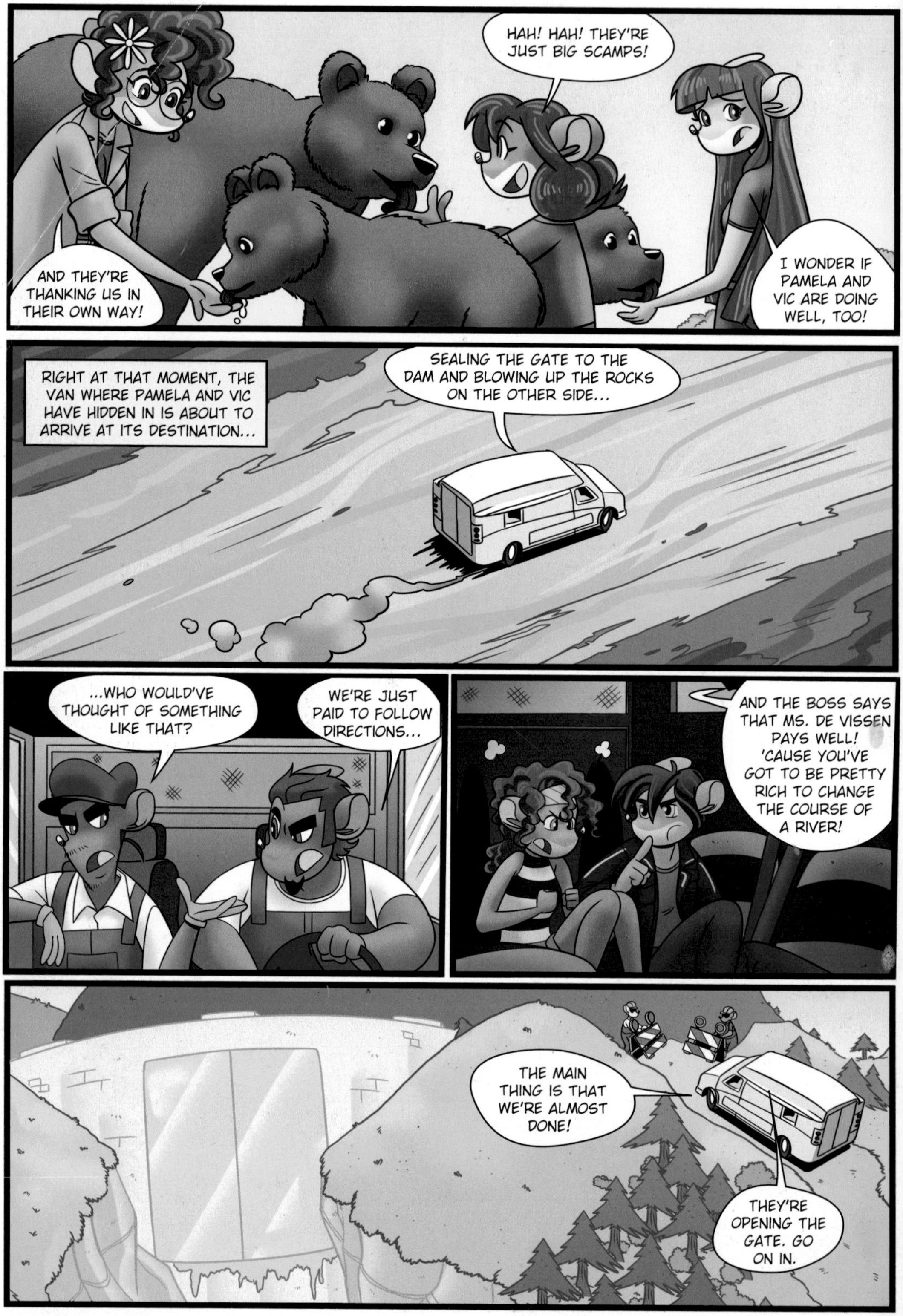
HAH! HAH! THEY'RE JUST BIG SCAMPS!
AND THEY'RE THANKING US IN THEIR OWN WAY!
I WONDER IF PAMELA AND VIC ARE DOING WELL, TOO!
RIGHT AT THAT MOMENT, THE VAN WHERE PAMELA AND VIC HAVE HIDDEN IN IS ABOUT TO ARRIVE AT ITS DESTINATION...
SEALING THE GATE TO THE DAM AND BLOWING UP THE ROCKS ON THE OTHER SIDE...
...WHO WOULD'VE THOUGHT OF SOMETHING LIKE THAT?
WE'RE JUST PAID TO FOLLOW DIRECTIONS...
AND THE BOSS SAYS THAT MS. DE VISSEN PAYS WELL! 'CAUSE YOU'VE GOT TO BE PRETTY RICH TO CHANGE THE COURSE OF A RIVER!
THE MAIN THING IS THAT WE'RE ALMOST DONE!
THEY'RE OPENING THE GATE. GO ON IN.

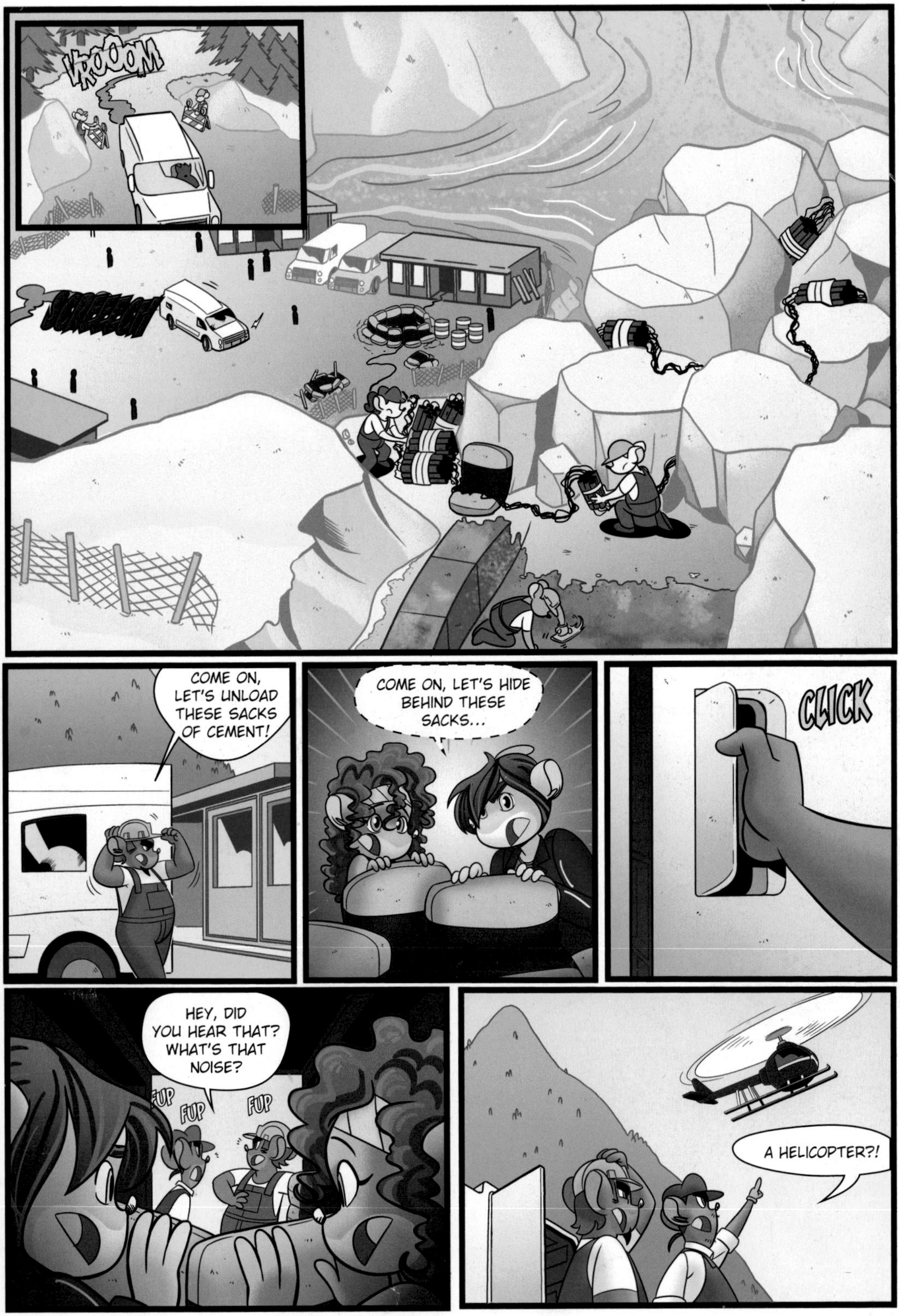
VROOOM
SCREEECH
COME ON, LET'S UNLOAD THESE SACKS OF CEMENT!
COME ON, LET'S HIDE BEHIND THESE SACKS...
CLICK
HEY, DID YOU HEAR THAT? WHAT'S THAT NOISE?
FUP
FUP
FUP
A HELICOPTER?!

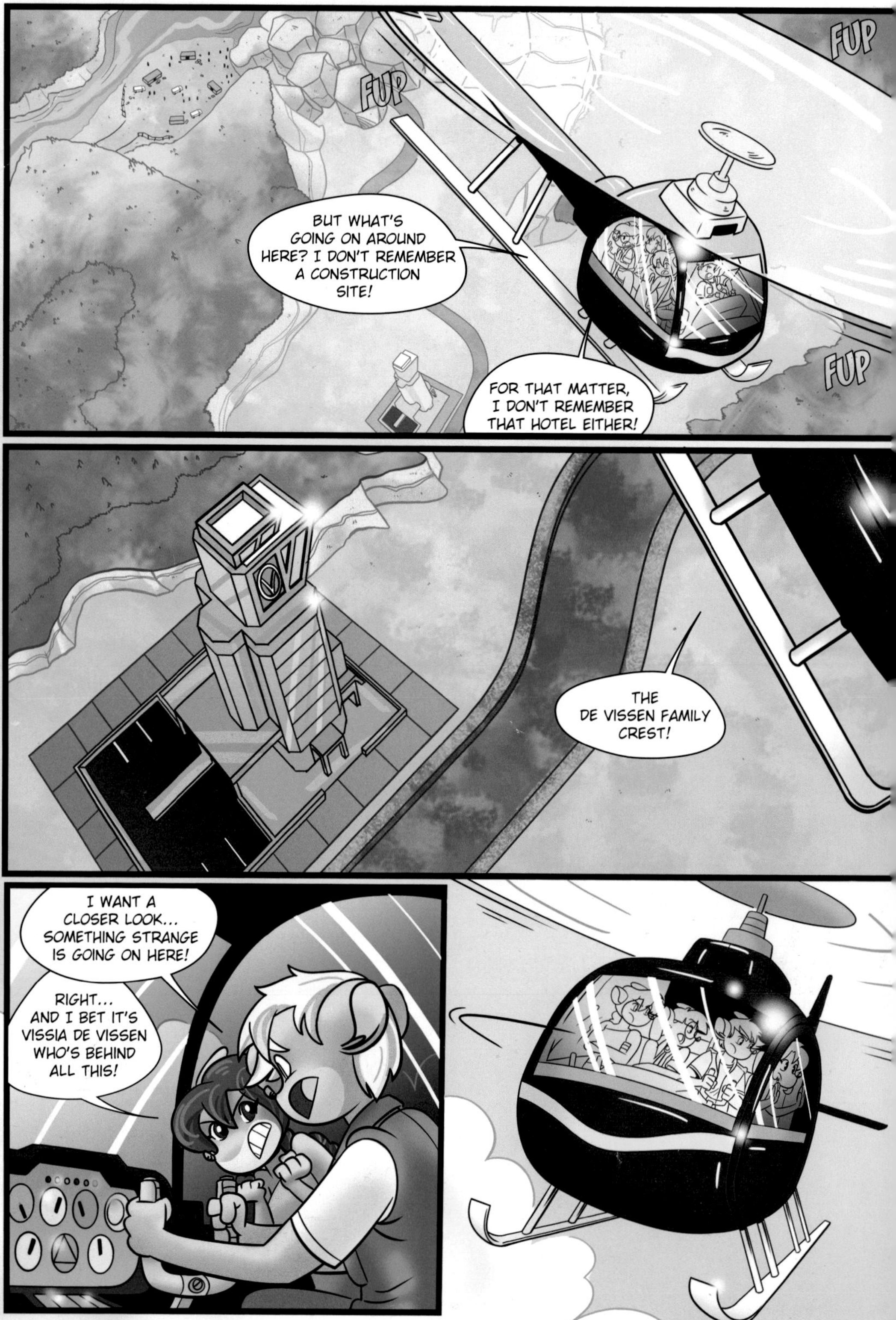
FUP
FUP
BUT WHAT'S GOING ON AROUND HERE? I DON'T REMEMBER A CONSTRUCTION SITE!
FOR THAT MATTER, I DON'T REMEMBER THAT HOTEL EITHER!
FUP
THE DE VISSEN FAMILY CREST!
I WANT A CLOSER LOOK... SOMETHING STRANGE IS GOING ON HERE!
RIGHT... AND I BET IT'S VISSIA DE VISSEN WHO'S BEHIND ALL THIS!

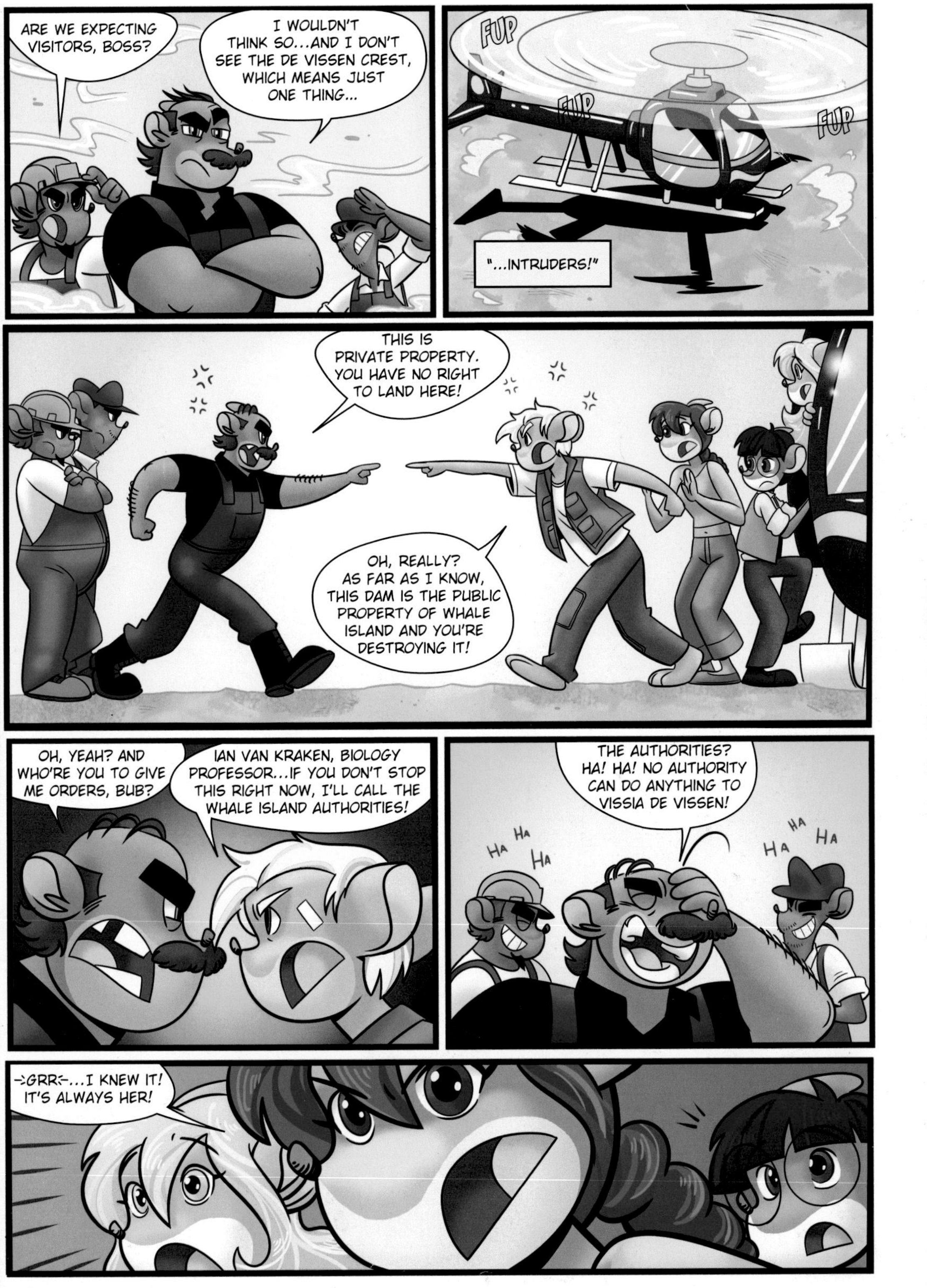
ARE WE EXPECTING VISITORS, BOSS?
I WOULDN'T THINK SO...AND I DON'T SEE THE DE VISSEN CREST, WHICH MEANS JUST ONE THING...
FUP
FUP
FUP
"...INTRUDERS!"
THIS IS PRIVATE PROPERTY. YOU HAVE NO RIGHT TO LAND HERE!
OH, REALLY? AS FAR AS I KNOW, THIS DAM IS THE PUBLIC PROPERTY OF WHALE ISLAND AND YOU'RE DESTROYING IT!
OH, YEAH? AND WHO'RE YOU TO GIVE ME ORDERS, BUB?
IAN VAN KRAKEN, BIOLOGY PROFESSOR...IF YOU DON'T STOP THIS RIGHT NOW, I'LL CALL THE WHALE ISLAND AUTHORITIES!
THE AUTHORITIES? HA! HA! NO AUTHORITY CAN DO ANYTHING TO VISSIA DE VISSEN!
HA HA HA
HA HA HA
GRR...I KNEW IT! IT'S ALWAYS HER!

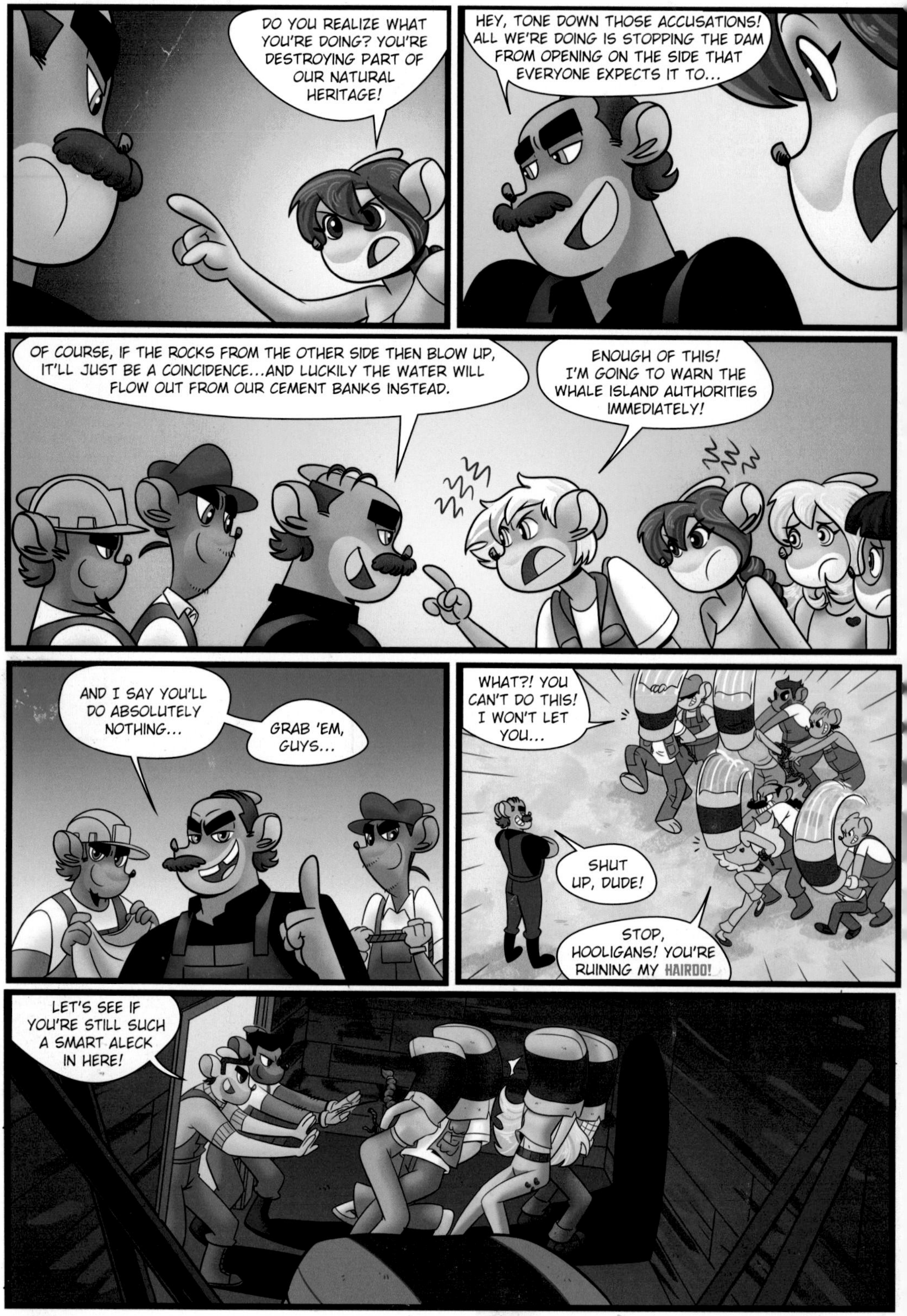
DO YOU REALIZE WHAT YOU'RE DOING? YOU'RE DESTROYING PART OF OUR NATURAL HERITAGE!
HEY, TONE DOWN THOSE ACCUSATIONS! ALL WE'RE DOING IS STOPPING THE DAM FROM OPENING ON THE SIDE THAT EVERYONE EXPECTS IT TO...
OF COURSE, IF THE ROCKS FROM THE OTHER SIDE THEN BLOW UP, IT'LL JUST BE A COINCIDENCE...AND LUCKILY THE WATER WILL FLOW OUT FROM OUR CEMENT BANKS INSTEAD.
ENOUGH OF THIS! I'M GOING TO WARN THE WHALE ISLAND AUTHORITIES IMMEDIATELY!
AND I SAY YOU'LL DO ABSOLUTELY NOTHING...
GRAB 'EM, GUYS...
WHAT?! YOU CAN'T DO THIS! I WON'T LET YOU...
SHUT UP, DUDE!
STOP, HOOLIGANS! YOU'RE RUINING MY HAIRDO!
LET'S SEE IF YOU'RE STILL SUCH A SMART ALECK IN HERE!

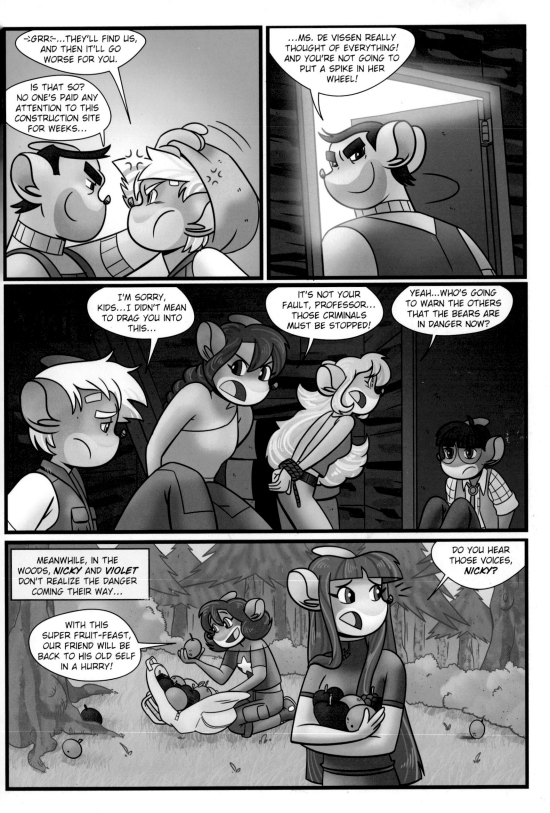

-:GRR:-...THEY'LL FIND US, AND THEN IT'LL GO WORSE FOR YOU.

IS THAT SO? NO ONE'S PAID ANY ATTENTION TO THIS CONSTRUCTION SITE FOR WEEKS...

...MS. DE VISSEN REALLY THOUGHT OF EVERYTHING! AND YOU'RE NOT GOING TO PUT A SPIKE IN HER WHEEL!

I'M SORRY, KIDS...I DIDN'T MEAN TO DRAG YOU INTO THIS...

IT'S NOT YOUR FAULT, PROFESSOR... THOSE CRIMINALS MUST BE STOPPED!

YEAH...WHO'S GOING TO WARN THE OTHERS THAT THE BEARS ARE IN DANGER NOW?

MEANWHILE, IN THE WOODS, NICKY AND VIOLET DON'T REALIZE THE DANGER COMING THEIR WAY...

DO YOU HEAR THOSE VOICES, NICKY?

WITH THIS SUPER FRUIT-FEAST, OUR FRIEND WILL BE BACK TO HIS OLD SELF IN A HURRY!

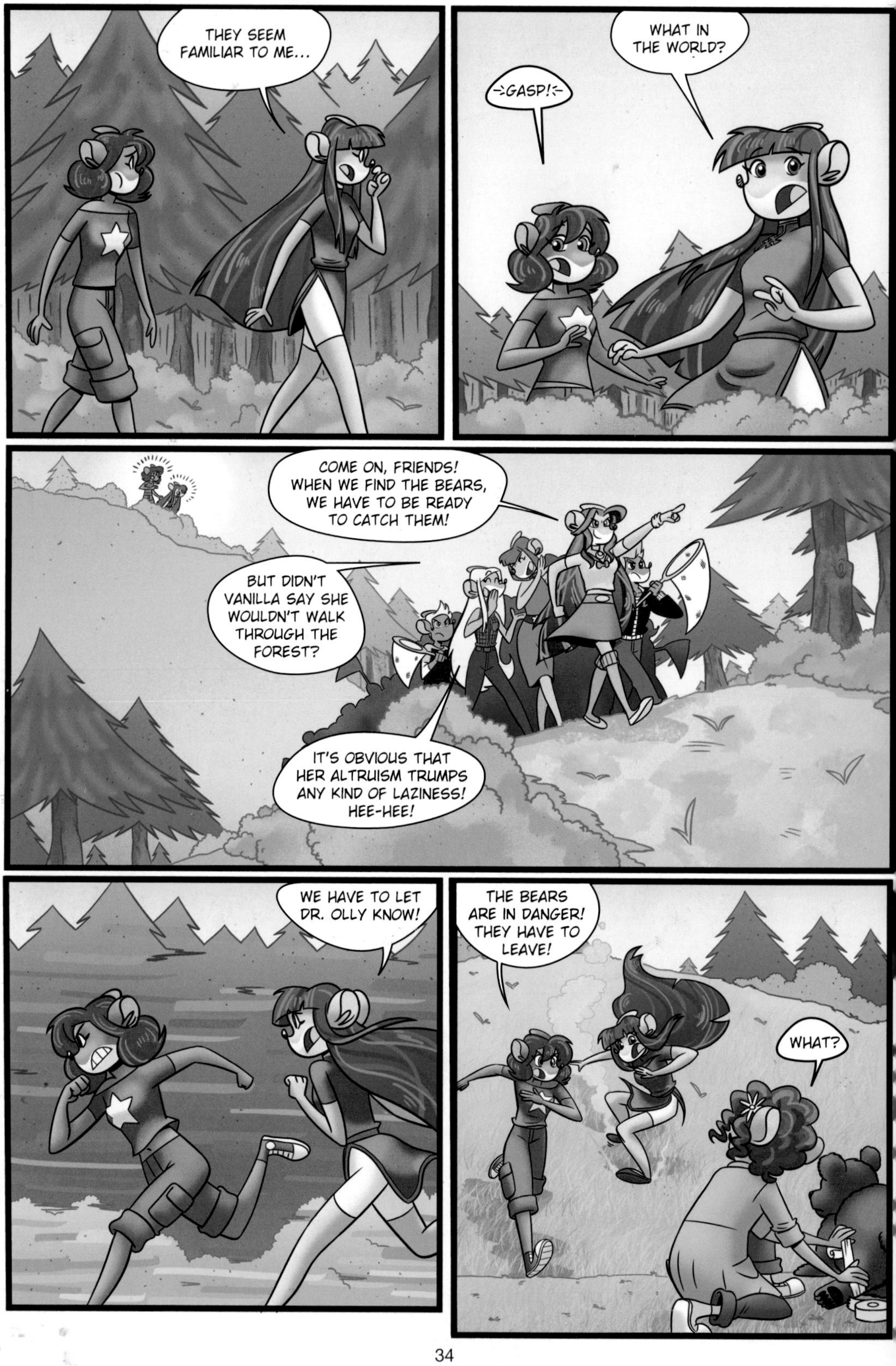
THEY SEEM FAMILIAR TO ME...
WHAT IN THE WORLD?
-GASP!-
COME ON, FRIENDS! WHEN WE FIND THE BEARS, WE HAVE TO BE READY TO CATCH THEM!
BUT DIDN'T VANILLA SAY SHE WOULDN'T WALK THROUGH THE FOREST?
IT'S OBVIOUS THAT HER ALTRUISM TRUMPS ANY KIND OF LAZINESS! HEE-HEE!
WE HAVE TO LET DR. OLLY KNOW!
THE BEARS ARE IN DANGER! THEY HAVE TO LEAVE!
WHAT?

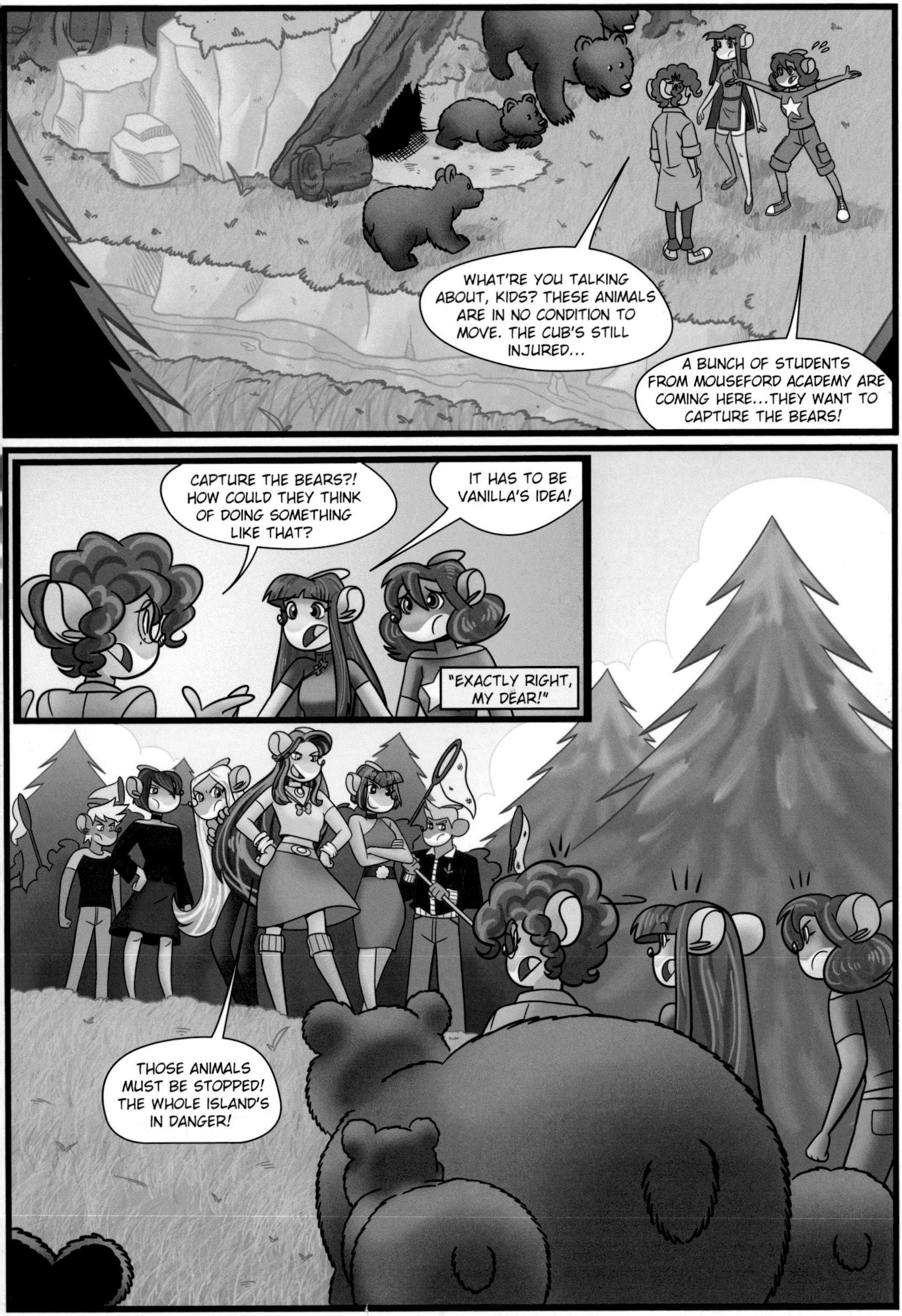
WHAT'RE YOU TALKING ABOUT, KIDS? THESE ANIMALS ARE IN NO CONDITION TO MOVE. THE CUB'S STILL INJURED...
A BUNCH OF STUDENTS FROM MOUSEFORD ACADEMY ARE COMING HERE...THEY WANT TO CAPTURE THE BEARS!
CAPTURE THE BEARS?! HOW COULD THEY THINK OF DOING SOMETHING LIKE THAT?
IT HAS TO BE VANILLA'S IDEA!
"EXACTLY RIGHT, MY DEAR!"
THOSE ANIMALS MUST BE STOPPED! THE WHOLE ISLAND'S IN DANGER!

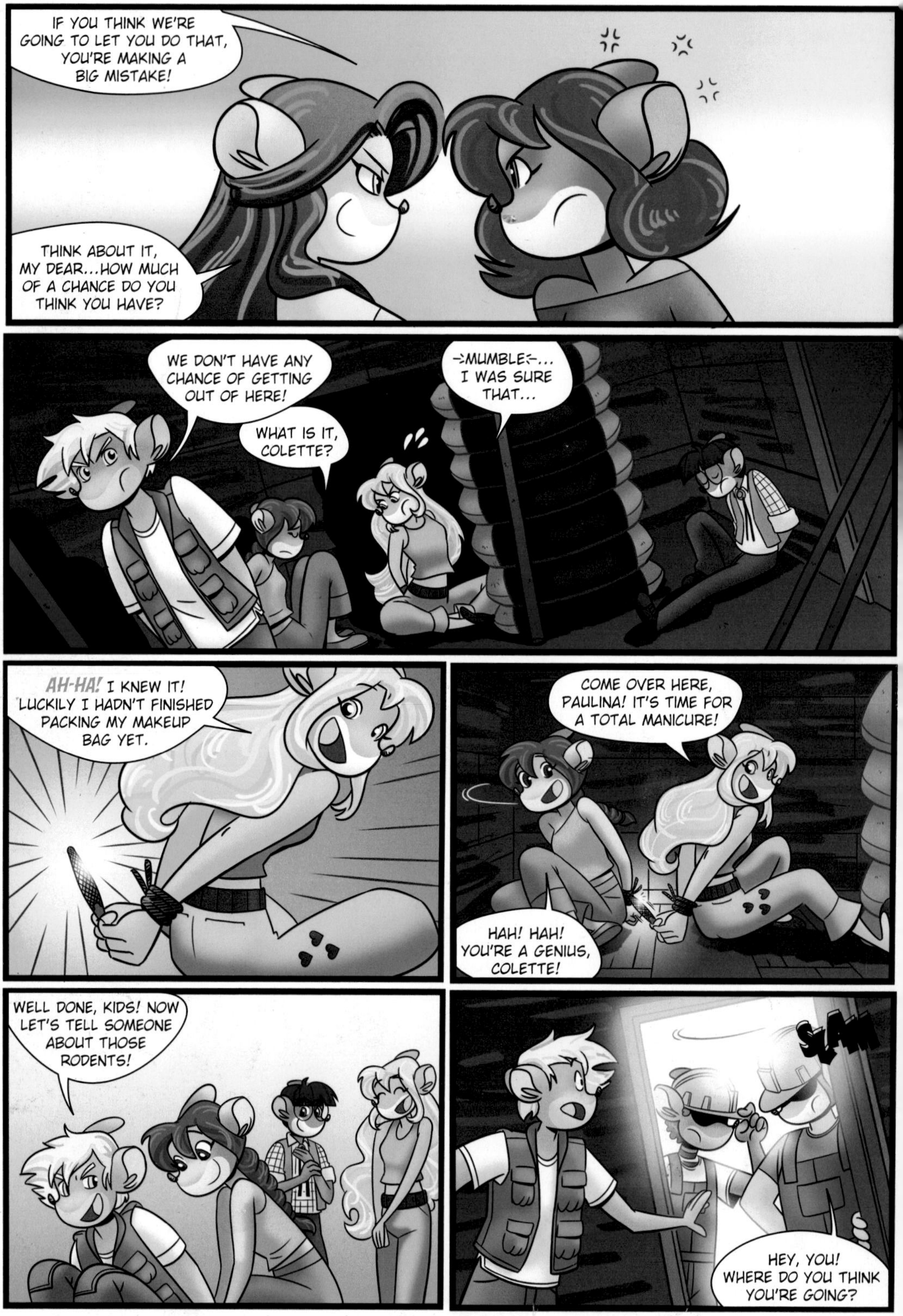
IF YOU THINK WE'RE GOING TO LET YOU DO THAT, YOU'RE MAKING A BIG MISTAKE!
THINK ABOUT IT, MY DEAR...HOW MUCH OF A CHANCE DO YOU THINK YOU HAVE?
WE DON'T HAVE ANY CHANCE OF GETTING OUT OF HERE!
WHAT IS IT, COLETTE?
~MUMBLE~... I WAS SURE THAT...
AH-HA! I KNEW IT! LUCKILY I HADN'T FINISHED PACKING MY MAKEUP BAG YET.
COME OVER HERE, PAULINA! IT'S TIME FOR A TOTAL MANICURE!
HAH! HAH! YOU'RE A GENIUS, COLETTE!
WELL DONE, KIDS! NOW LET'S TELL SOMEONE ABOUT THOSE RODENTS!
SLAM
HEY, YOU! WHERE DO YOU THINK YOU'RE GOING?

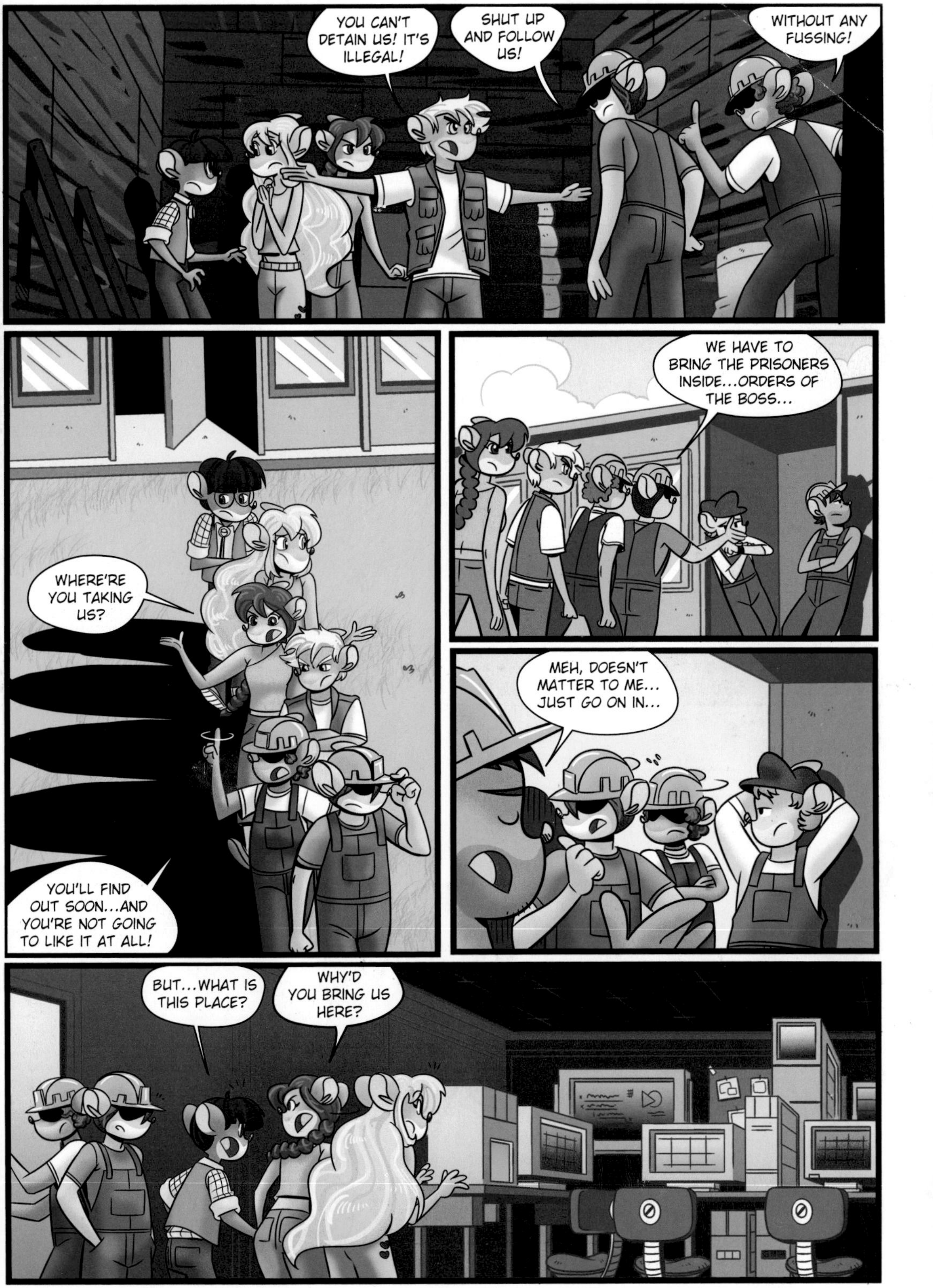
YOU CAN'T DETAIN US! IT'S ILLEGAL!
SHUT UP AND FOLLOW US!
WITHOUT ANY FUSSING!
WHERE'RE YOU TAKING US?
YOU'LL FIND OUT SOON...AND YOU'RE NOT GOING TO LIKE IT AT ALL!
WE HAVE TO BRING THE PRISONERS INSIDE...ORDERS OF THE BOSS...
MEH, DOESN'T MATTER TO ME... JUST GO ON IN...
BUT...WHAT IS THIS PLACE?
WHY'D YOU BRING US HERE?

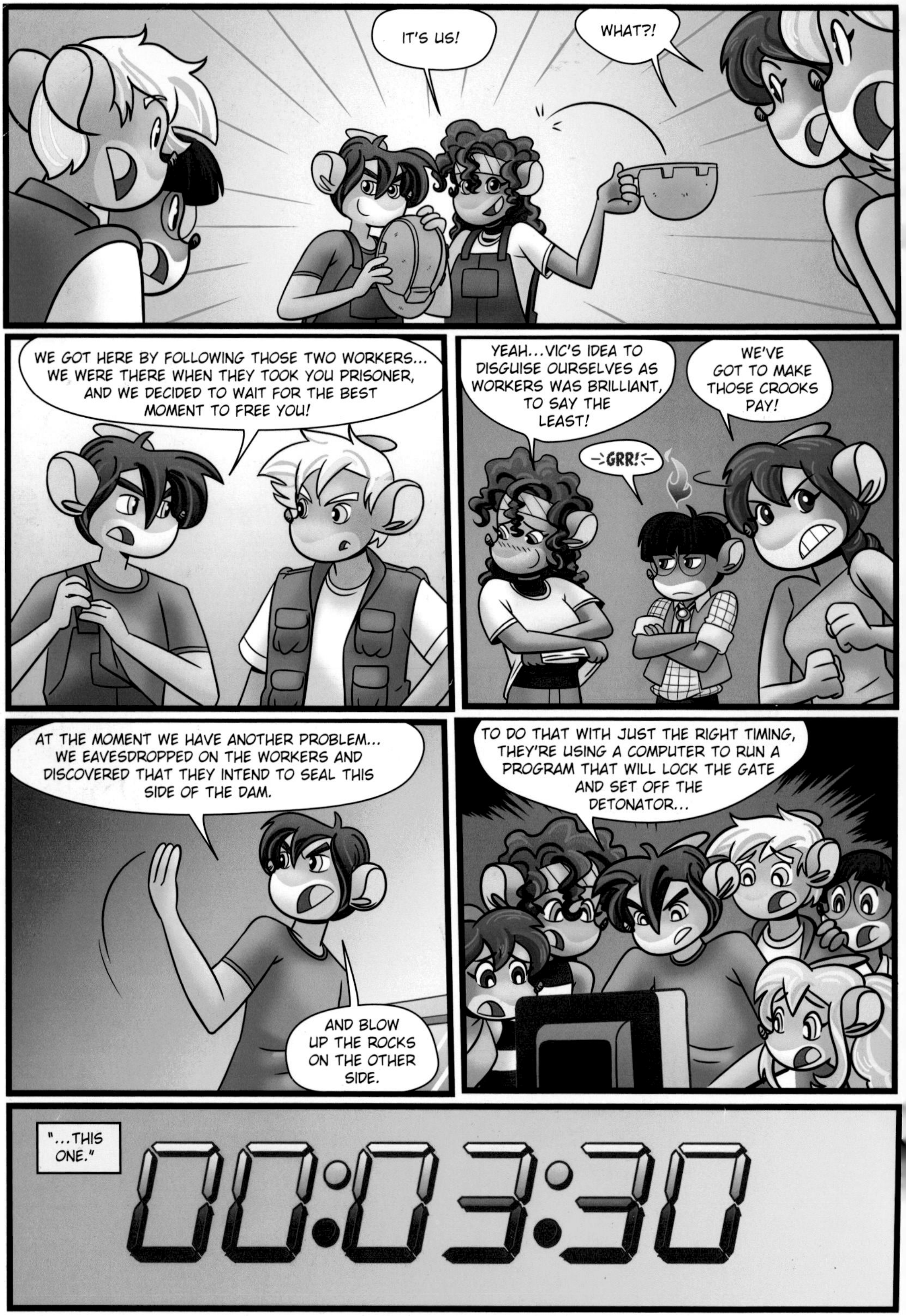
IT'S US!
WHAT?!
WE GOT HERE BY FOLLOWING THOSE TWO WORKERS... WE WERE THERE WHEN THEY TOOK YOU PRISONER, AND WE DECIDED TO WAIT FOR THE BEST MOMENT TO FREE YOU!
YEAH...VIC'S IDEA TO DISGUISE OURSELVES AS WORKERS WAS BRILLIANT, TO SAY THE LEAST!
WE'VE GOT TO MAKE THOSE CROOKS PAY!
GRR!
AT THE MOMENT WE HAVE ANOTHER PROBLEM... WE EAVESDROPPED ON THE WORKERS AND DISCOVERED THAT THEY INTEND TO SEAL THIS SIDE OF THE DAM.
AND BLOW UP THE ROCKS ON THE OTHER SIDE.
TO DO THAT WITH JUST THE RIGHT TIMING, THEY'RE USING A COMPUTER TO RUN A PROGRAM THAT WILL LOCK THE GATE AND SET OFF THE DETONATOR...
"...THIS ONE."
00:03:30

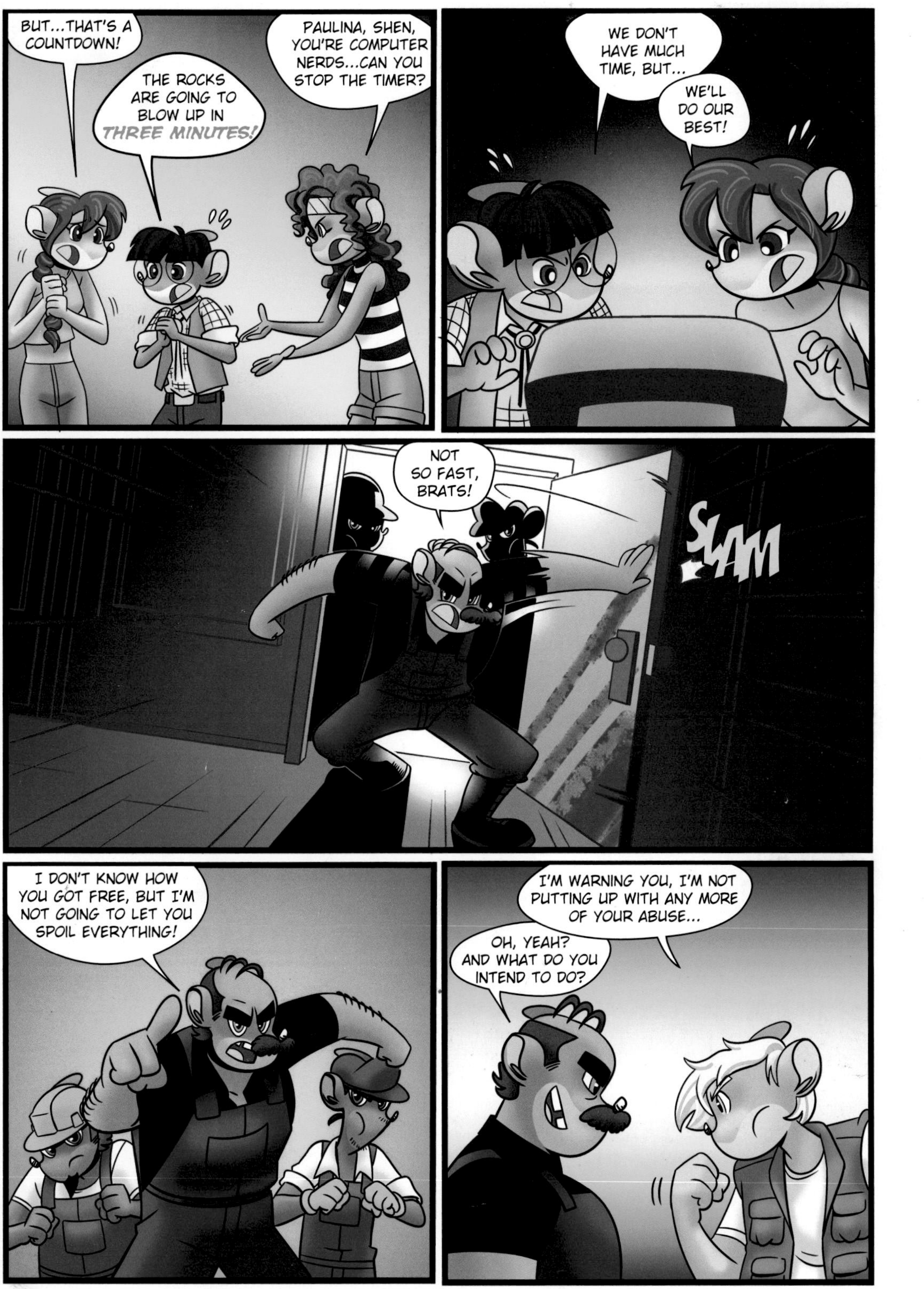

BUT...THAT'S A COUNTDOWN!
THE ROCKS ARE GOING TO BLOW UP IN THREE MINUTES!
PAULINA, SHEN, YOU'RE COMPUTER NERDS...CAN YOU STOP THE TIMER?
WE DON'T HAVE MUCH TIME, BUT...
WE'LL DO OUR BEST!
NOT SO FAST, BRATS!
SLAM
I DON'T KNOW HOW YOU GOT FREE, BUT I'M NOT GOING TO LET YOU SPOIL EVERYTHING!
I'M WARNING YOU, I'M NOT PUTTING UP WITH ANY MORE OF YOUR ABUSE...
OH, YEAH? AND WHAT DO YOU INTEND TO DO?

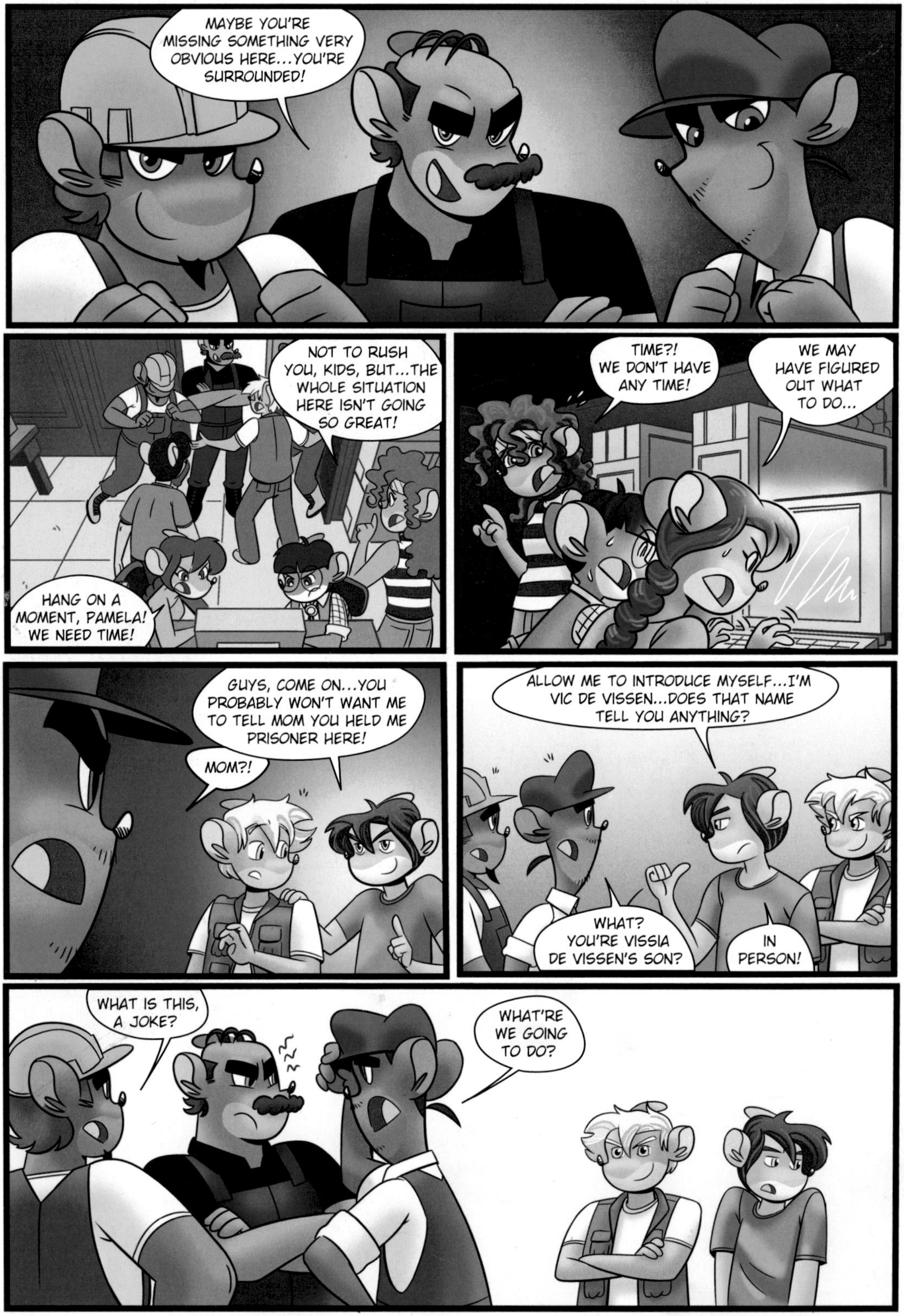
MAYBE YOU'RE MISSING SOMETHING VERY OBVIOUS HERE...YOU'RE SURROUNDED!
NOT TO RUSH YOU, KIDS, BUT...THE WHOLE SITUATION HERE ISN'T GOING SO GREAT!
HANG ON A MOMENT, PAMELA! WE NEED TIME!
TIME?! WE DON'T HAVE ANY TIME!
WE MAY HAVE FIGURED OUT WHAT TO DO...
GUYS, COME ON...YOU PROBABLY WON'T WANT ME TO TELL MOM YOU HELD ME PRISONER HERE!
MOM?!
ALLOW ME TO INTRODUCE MYSELF...I'M VIC DE VISSEN...DOES THAT NAME TELL YOU ANYTHING?
WHAT? YOU'RE VISSIA DE VISSEN'S SON?
IN PERSON!
WHAT IS THIS, A JOKE?
WHAT'RE WE GOING TO DO?

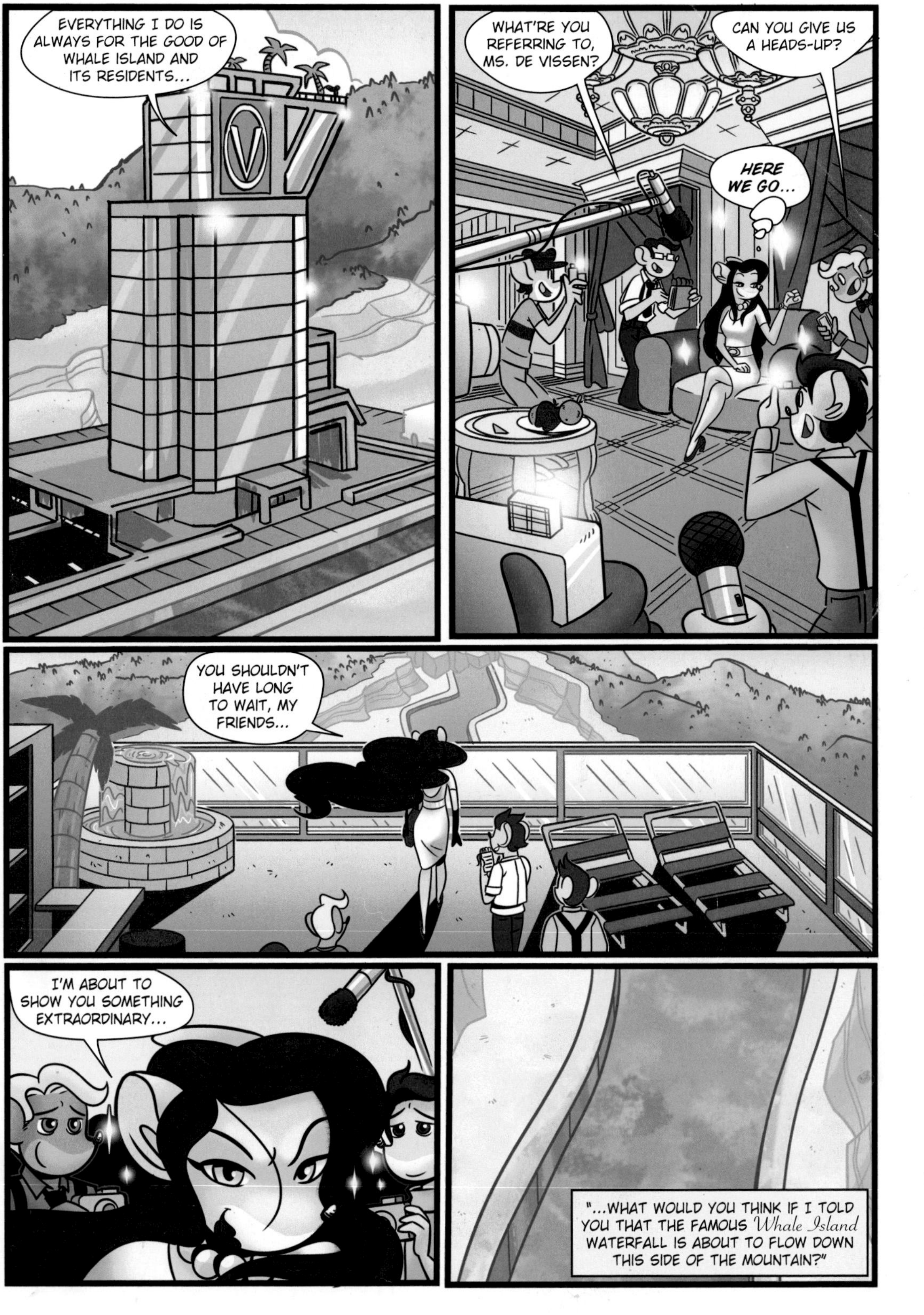
EVERYTHING I DO IS ALWAYS FOR THE GOOD OF WHALE ISLAND AND ITS RESIDENTS...
WHAT'RE YOU REFERRING TO, MS. DE VISSEN?
CAN YOU GIVE US A HEADS-UP?
HERE WE GO...
YOU SHOULDN'T HAVE LONG TO WAIT, MY FRIENDS...
I'M ABOUT TO SHOW YOU SOMETHING EXTRAORDINARY...
"...WHAT WOULD YOU THINK IF I TOLD YOU THAT THE FAMOUS Whale Island WATERFALL IS ABOUT TO FLOW DOWN THIS SIDE OF THE MOUNTAIN?"

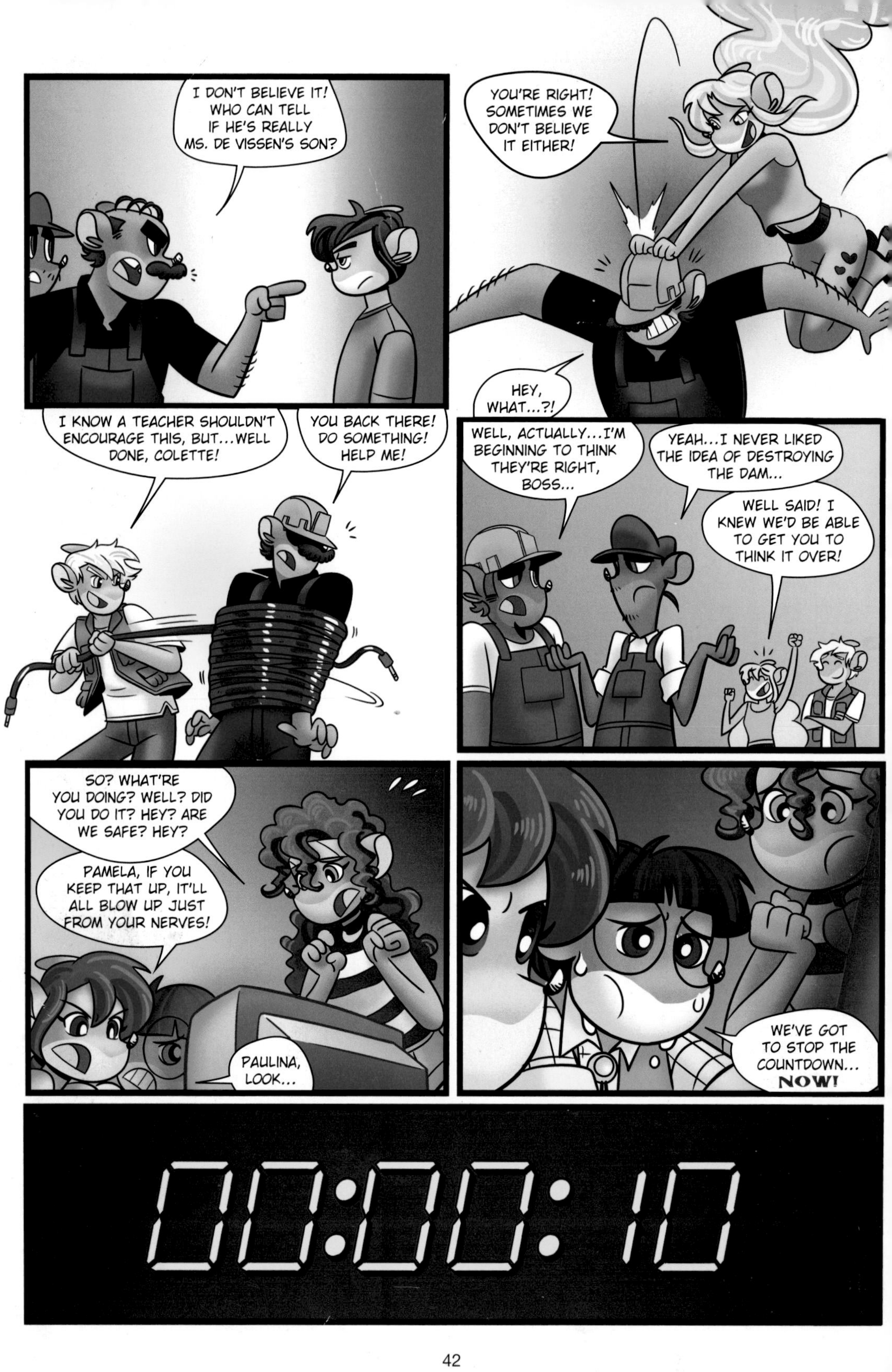

I DON'T BELIEVE IT! WHO CAN TELL IF HE'S REALLY MS. DE VISSEN'S SON?
YOU'RE RIGHT! SOMETIMES WE DON'T BELIEVE IT EITHER!
HEY, WHAT...?!
I KNOW A TEACHER SHOULDN'T ENCOURAGE THIS, BUT...WELL DONE, COLETTE!
YOU BACK THERE! DO SOMETHING! HELP ME!
WELL, ACTUALLY...I'M BEGINNING TO THINK THEY'RE RIGHT, BOSS...
YEAH...I NEVER LIKED THE IDEA OF DESTROYING THE DAM...
WELL SAID! I KNEW WE'D BE ABLE TO GET YOU TO THINK IT OVER!
SO? WHAT'RE YOU DOING? WELL? DID YOU DO IT? HEY? ARE WE SAFE? HEY?
PAMELA, IF YOU KEEP THAT UP, IT'LL ALL BLOW UP JUST FROM YOUR NERVES!
PAULINA, LOOK...
WE'VE GOT TO STOP THE COUNTDOWN... NOW!
00:00:10

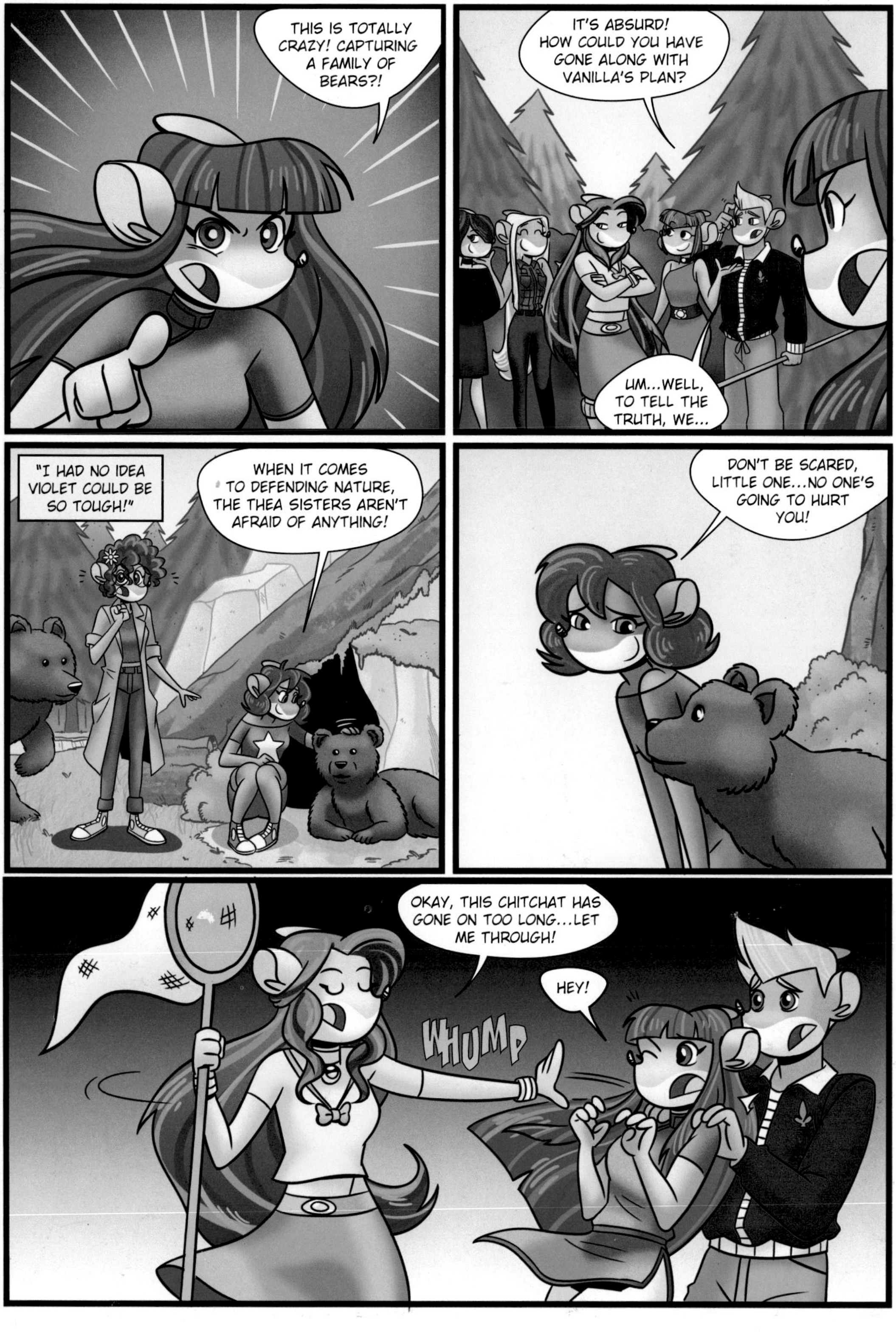

THIS IS TOTALLY CRAZY! CAPTURING A FAMILY OF BEARS?!
IT'S ABSURD! HOW COULD YOU HAVE GONE ALONG WITH VANILLA'S PLAN?
UM...WELL, TO TELL THE TRUTH, WE...
"I HAD NO IDEA VIOLET COULD BE SO TOUGH!"
WHEN IT COMES TO DEFENDING NATURE, THE THEA SISTERS AREN'T AFRAID OF ANYTHING!
DON'T BE SCARED, LITTLE ONE...NO ONE'S GOING TO HURT YOU!
OKAY, THIS CHITCHAT HAS GONE ON TOO LONG...LET ME THROUGH!
HEY!
WHUMP

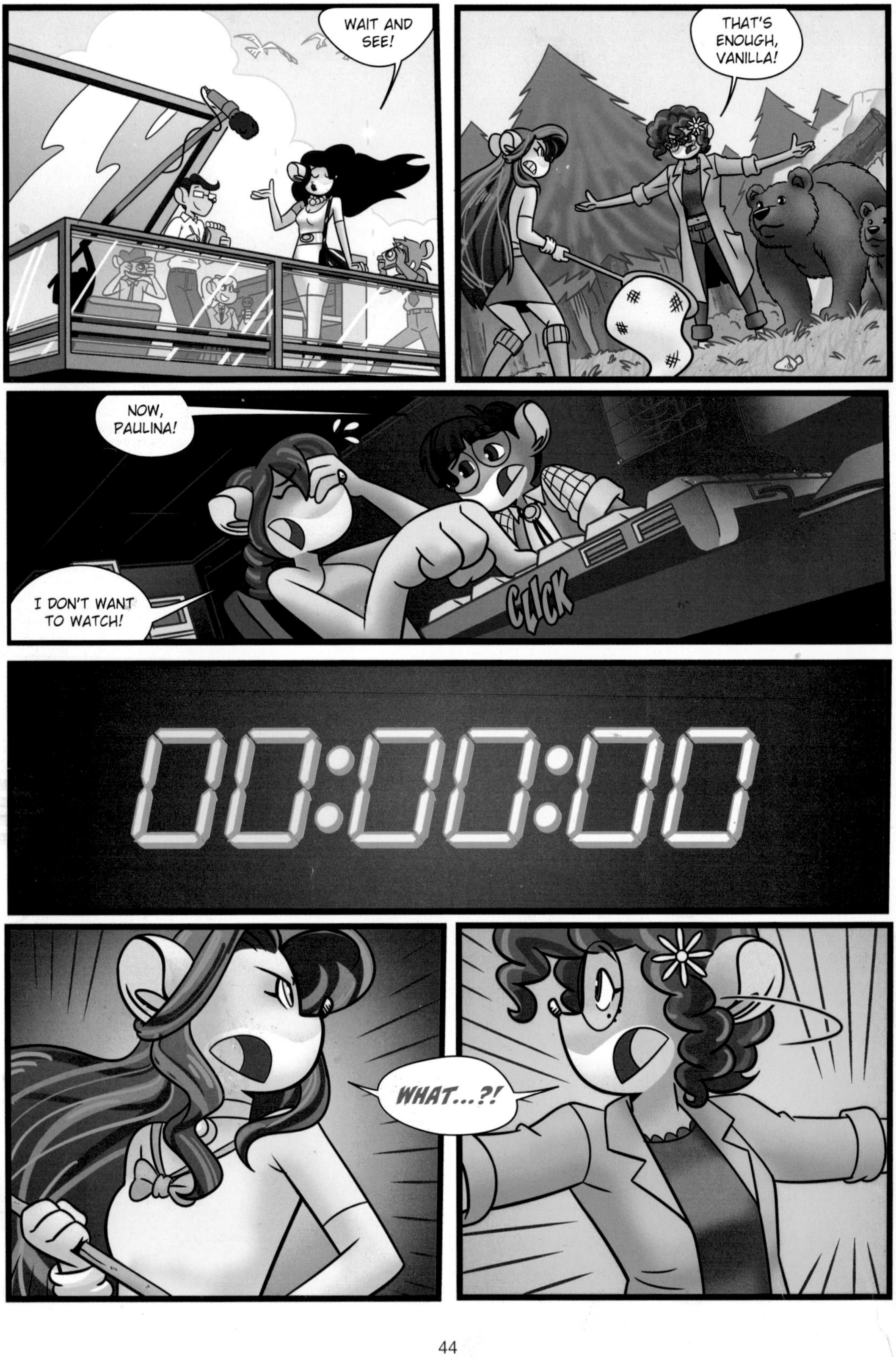
WAIT AND SEE!
THAT'S ENOUGH, VANILLA!
NOW, PAULINA!
I DON'T WANT TO WATCH!
CLICK
00:00:00
WHAT...?!

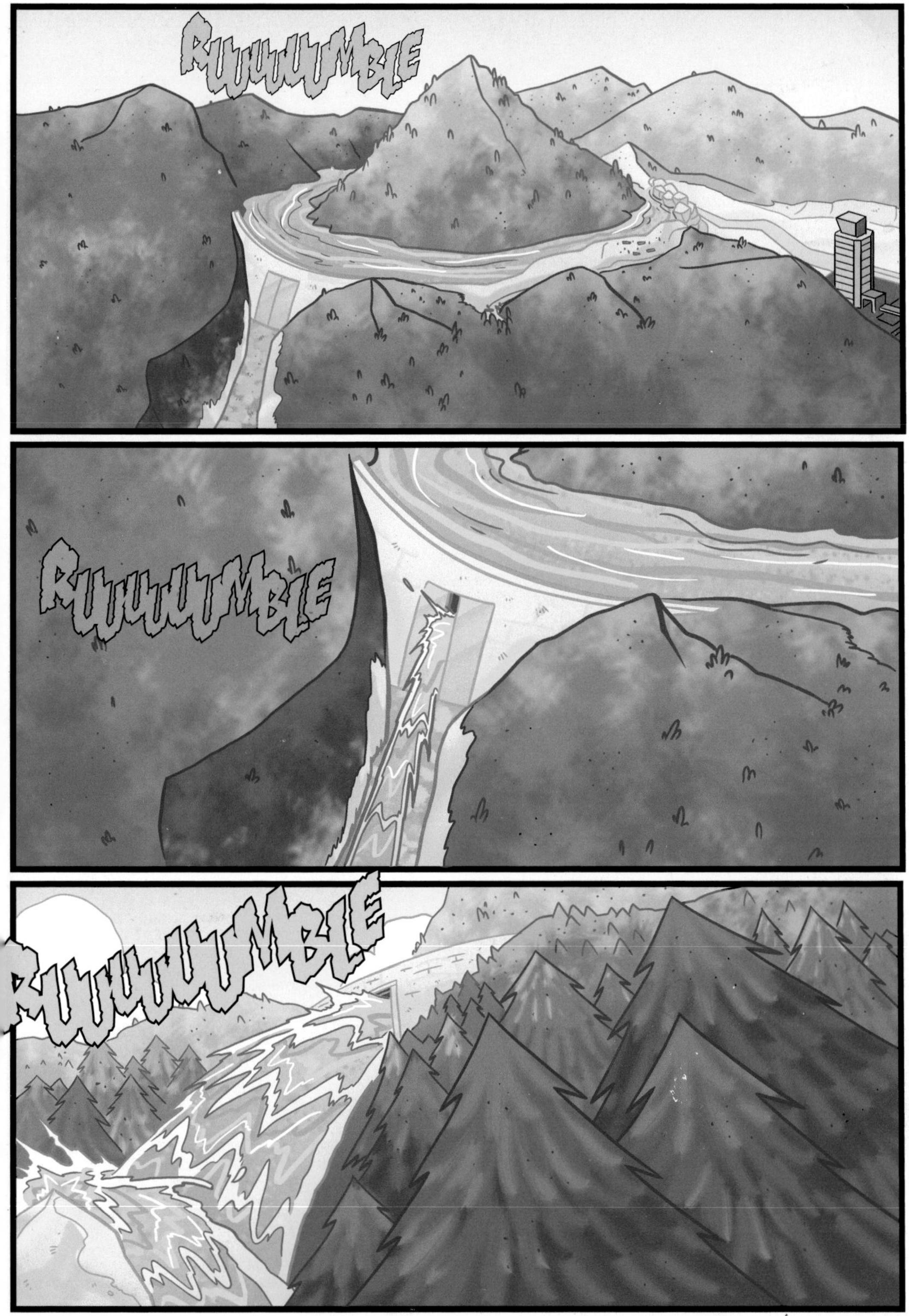
RUUUUUMBLE
RUUUUUMBLE
RUUUUUMBLE

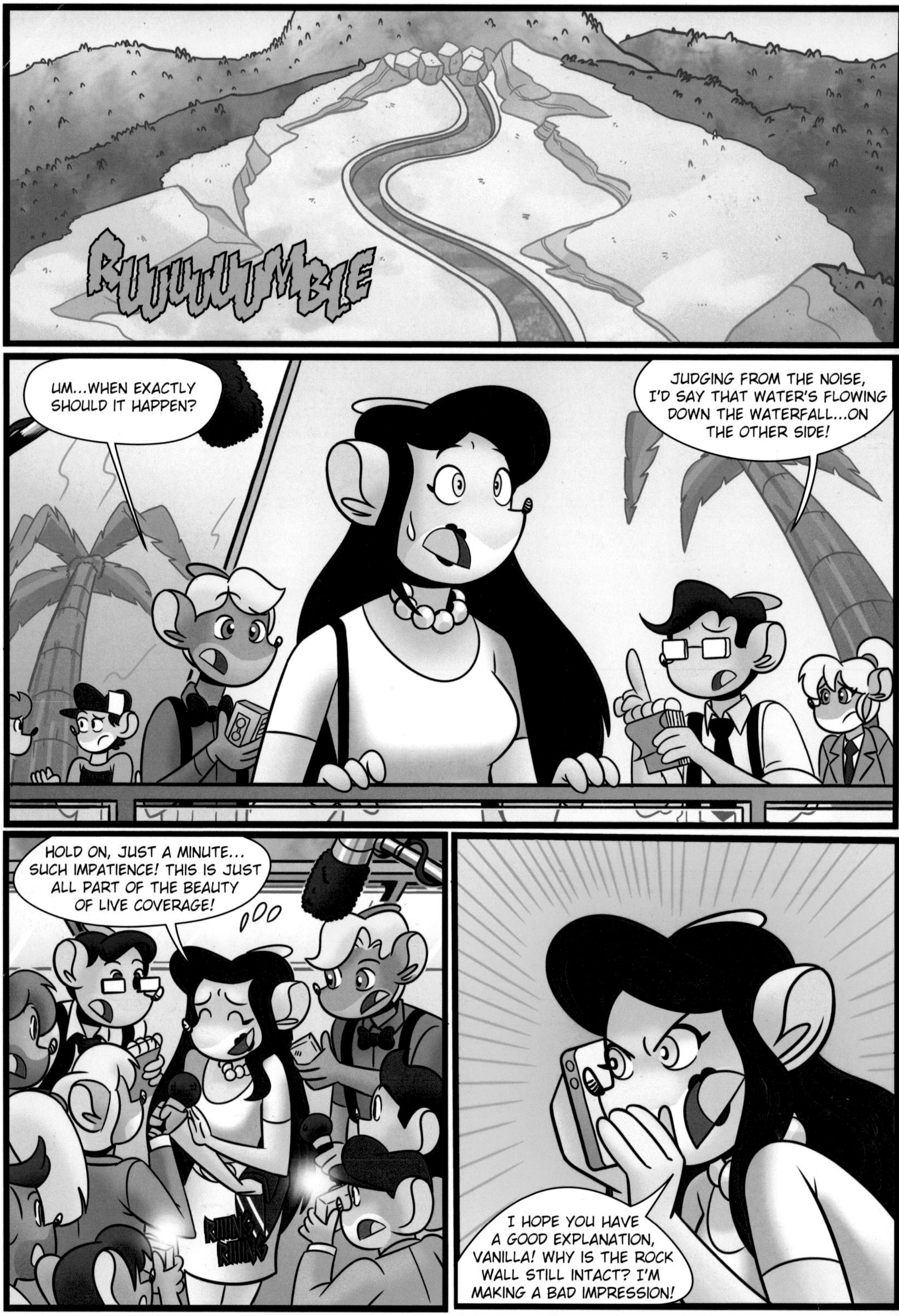
RUUUUUMBLE
UM...WHEN EXACTLY SHOULD IT HAPPEN?
JUDGING FROM THE NOISE, I'D SAY THAT WATER'S FLOWING DOWN THE WATERFALL...ON THE OTHER SIDE!
HOLD ON, JUST A MINUTE... SUCH IMPATIENCE! THIS IS JUST ALL PART OF THE BEAUTY OF LIVE COVERAGE!
I HOPE YOU HAVE A GOOD EXPLANATION, VANILLA! WHY IS THE ROCK WALL STILL INTACT? I'M MAKING A BAD IMPRESSION!

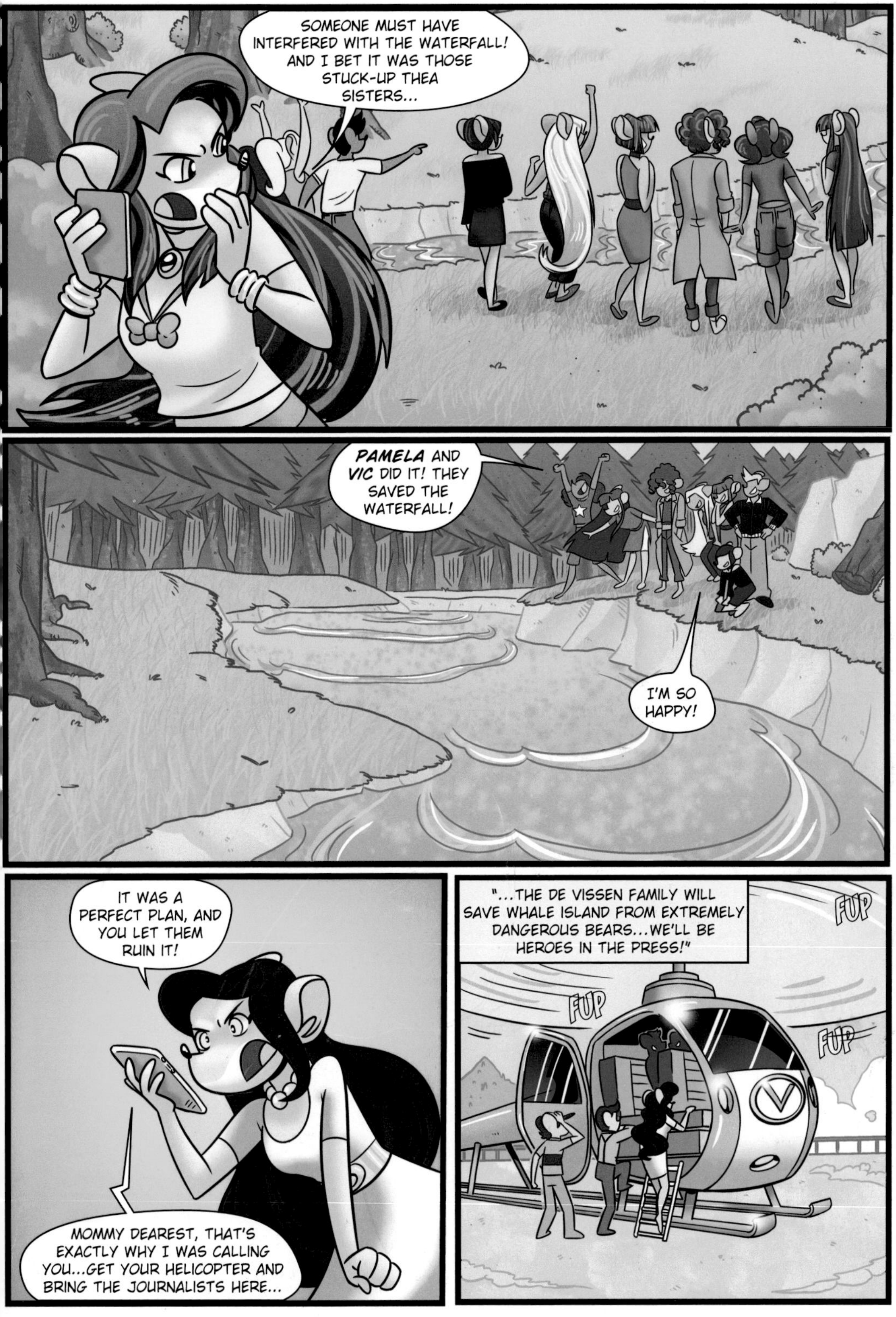
SOMEONE MUST HAVE INTERFERED WITH THE WATERFALL! AND I BET IT WAS THOSE STUCK-UP THEA SISTERS...
PAMELA AND VIC DID IT! THEY SAVED THE WATERFALL!
I'M SO HAPPY!
IT WAS A PERFECT PLAN, AND YOU LET THEM RUIN IT!
MOMMY DEAREST, THAT'S EXACTLY WHY I WAS CALLING YOU...GET YOUR HELICOPTER AND BRING THE JOURNALISTS HERE...
"...THE DE VISSEN FAMILY WILL SAVE WHALE ISLAND FROM EXTREMELY DANGEROUS BEARS...WE'LL BE HEROES IN THE PRESS!"
FUP
FUP
FUP

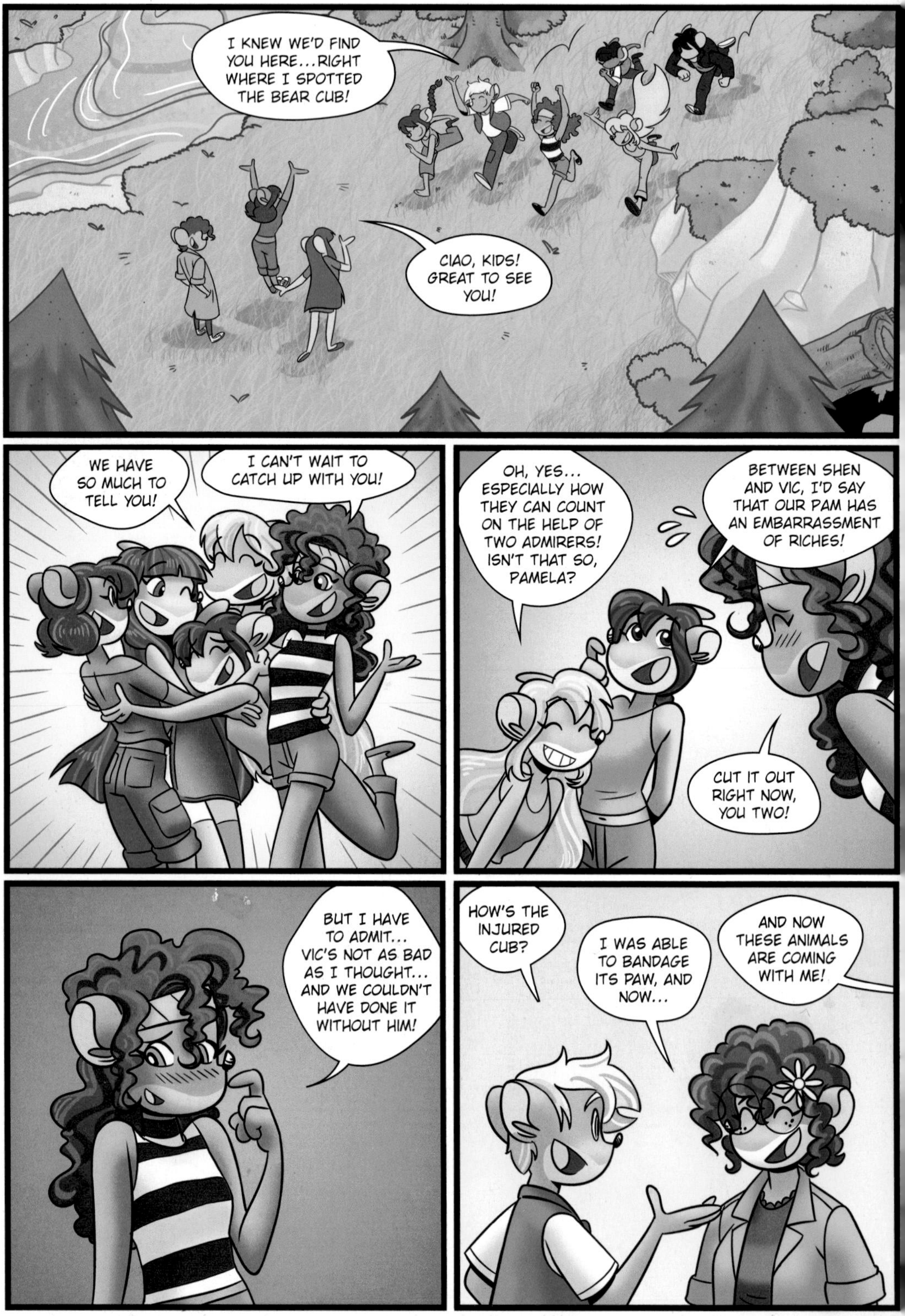
I KNEW WE'D FIND YOU HERE...RIGHT WHERE I SPOTTED THE BEAR CUB!
CIAO, KIDS! GREAT TO SEE YOU!
WE HAVE SO MUCH TO TELL YOU!
I CAN'T WAIT TO CATCH UP WITH YOU!
OH, YES... ESPECIALLY HOW THEY CAN COUNT ON THE HELP OF TWO ADMIRERS! ISN'T THAT SO, PAMELA?
BETWEEN SHEN AND VIC, I'D SAY THAT OUR PAM HAS AN EMBARRASSMENT OF RICHES!
CUT IT OUT RIGHT NOW, YOU TWO!
BUT I HAVE TO ADMIT... VIC'S NOT AS BAD AS I THOUGHT... AND WE COULDN'T HAVE DONE IT WITHOUT HIM!
HOW'S THE INJURED CUB?
I WAS ABLE TO BANDAGE ITS PAW, AND NOW...
AND NOW THESE ANIMALS ARE COMING WITH ME!

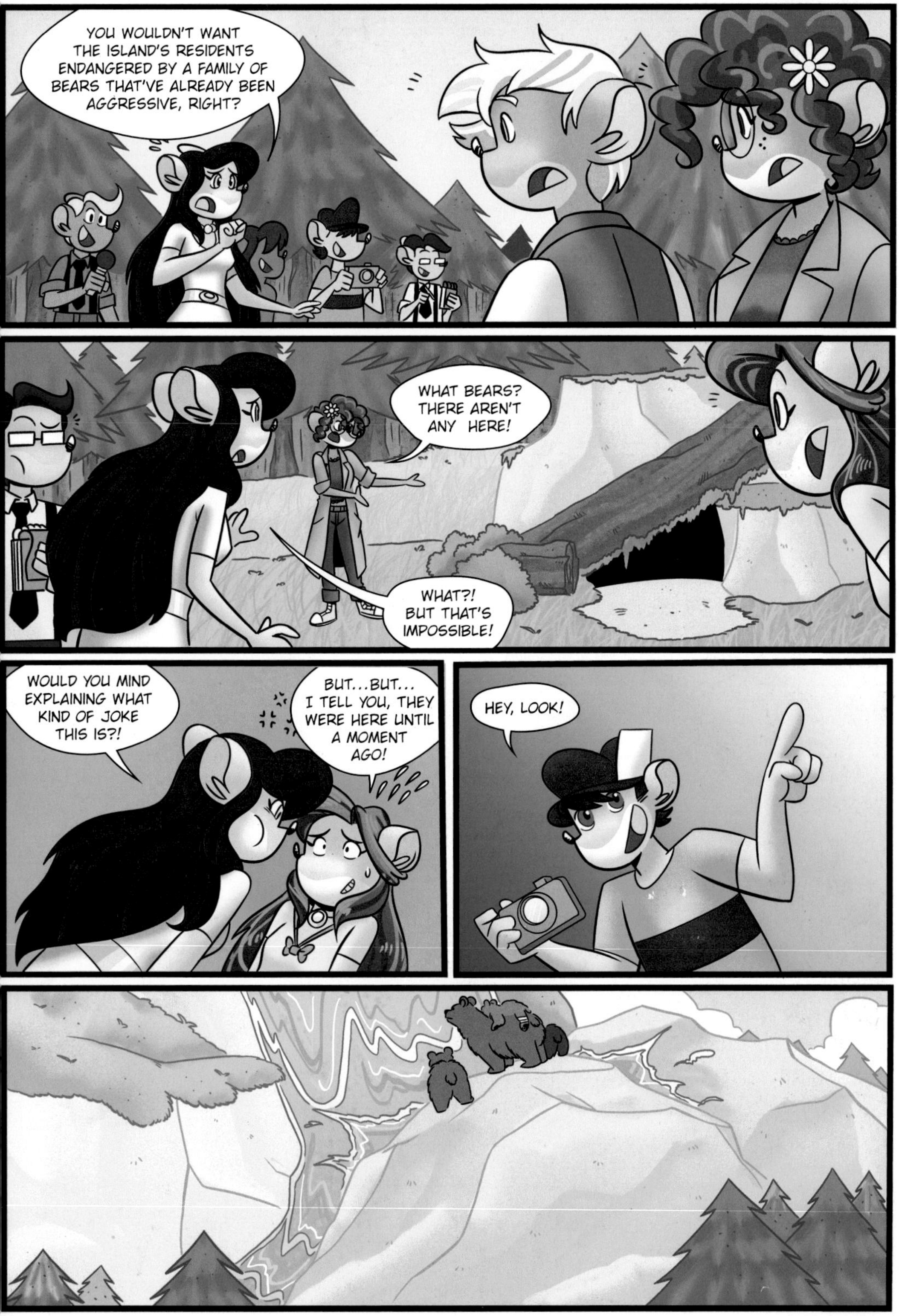
YOU WOULDN'T WANT THE ISLAND'S RESIDENTS ENDANGERED BY A FAMILY OF BEARS THAT'VE ALREADY BEEN AGGRESSIVE, RIGHT?
WHAT BEARS? THERE AREN'T ANY HERE!
WHAT?! BUT THAT'S IMPOSSIBLE!
WOULD YOU MIND EXPLAINING WHAT KIND OF JOKE THIS IS?!
BUT...BUT... I TELL YOU, THEY WERE HERE UNTIL A MOMENT AGO!
HEY, LOOK!

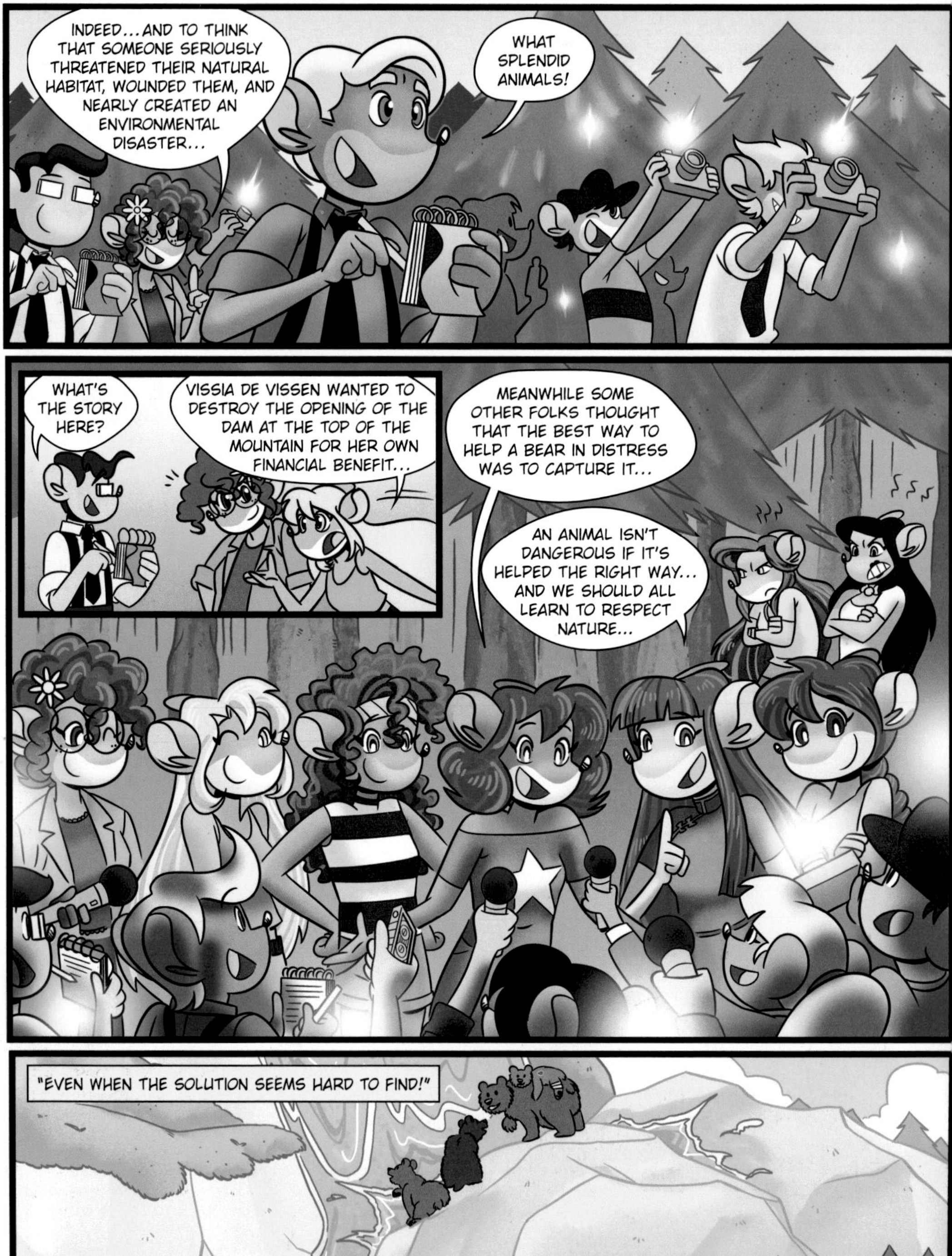
INDEED... AND TO THINK THAT SOMEONE SERIOUSLY THREATENED THEIR NATURAL HABITAT, WOUNDED THEM, AND NEARLY CREATED AN ENVIRONMENTAL DISASTER...
WHAT SPLENDID ANIMALS!
WHAT'S THE STORY HERE?
VISSIA DE VISSEN WANTED TO DESTROY THE OPENING OF THE DAM AT THE TOP OF THE MOUNTAIN FOR HER OWN FINANCIAL BENEFIT...
MEANWHILE SOME OTHER FOLKS THOUGHT THAT THE BEST WAY TO HELP A BEAR IN DISTRESS WAS TO CAPTURE IT...
AN ANIMAL ISN'T DANGEROUS IF IT'S HELPED THE RIGHT WAY... AND WE SHOULD ALL LEARN TO RESPECT NATURE...
"EVEN WHEN THE SOLUTION SEEMS HARD TO FIND!"
[redacted]

Watch Out For PAPERCUTZ™

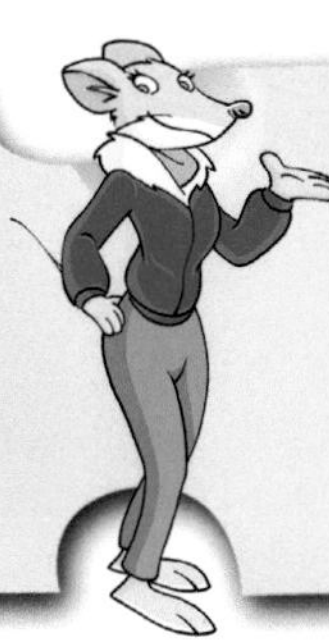

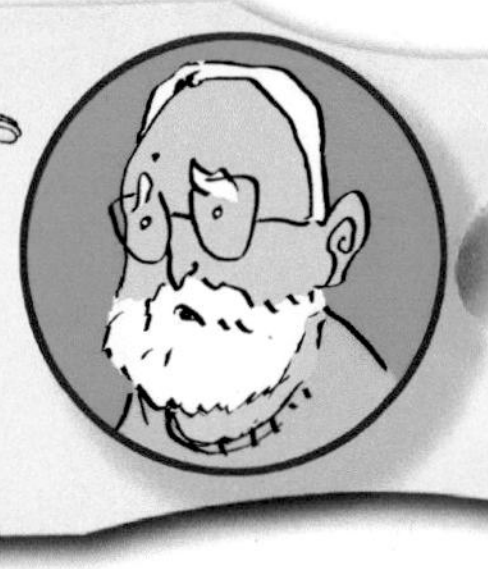

'elcome to the fun-filled, eco-friendly fifth THEA STILTON graphic novel from Papercutz, those cheese-loving folks edicated to publishing great graphic novels for all ages. I'm *Jim Salicrup,* Editor-in-Cheese, er, I mean, Chief and Honorary ditor of the Mouseford Academy Yearbook.

s much fun as this particular graphic novel may be, did you know there's even more THEA STILTON and Papercutz xcitement waiting for you online? Just head on over to geronimostilton.com and you'll find all sorts of stuff about Thea tilton and her cousin Geronimo Stilton—as well as an awesome app that can mousify your photos. While over at Papercutz. om there's a ton of information about such Papercutz projects as...

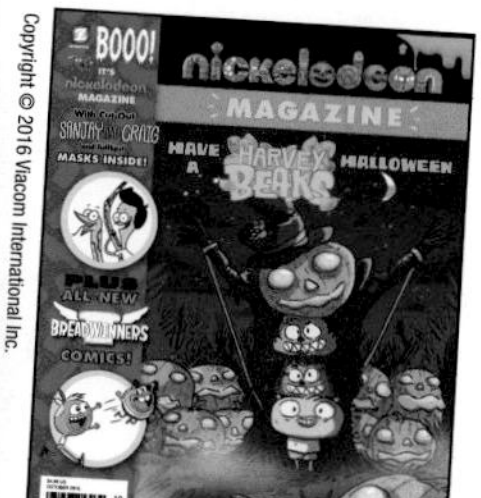

BOOO!
nickelodeon
MAGAZINE
SANJAY AND CRAIG
MASKS INSIDE!
HAVE A HARVEY BEAKS HALLOWEEN
PLUS ALL NEW BREADWINNERS COMICS!

NICKELODEON MAGAZINE - an all-new, all-different magazine filled with comics based on the newest stars seen on Nickelodeon. There's Sanjay and Craig, Breadwinners, Harvey Beaks and Pig Goat Banana Cricket! The same cartoon superstars who are now appearing on Friday nights on Nickelodeon also star in this awesome magazine. (Even Geronimo Stilton made a surprise cameo appearance in the Calendar in the October issue!) You'll find information on how to subscribe to the magazine on the site, or you can just visit your favorite newsstand or wherever they sell magazines and check out the latest issue.

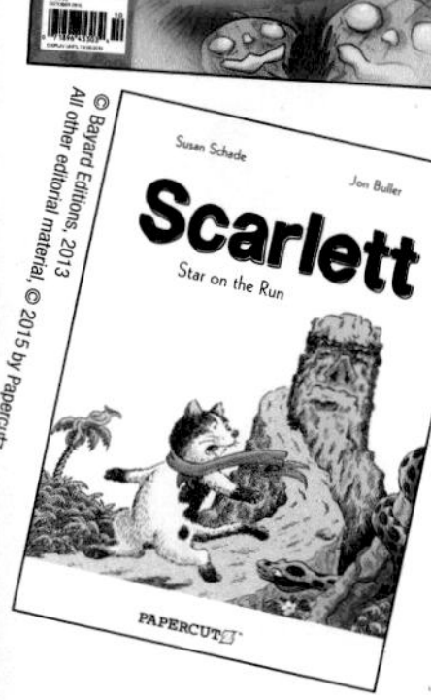

Susan Schade
Jon Buller
Scarlett
Star on the Run
PAPERCUTZ

SCARLETT - an exciting graphic novel that's half graphic novel, half chapter book. Scarlett is a small, harlequin-colored cat—that's right, a cat!—and a huge movie star. And what's more—she talks! Abused by her producer, however, she dreams of only one thing: escaping! So, when the occasion presents itself, she runs for her life. In the company of Trotter, a dog who's escaped the same torment, she is taken in by Mr. Frank Mole. But with the noose getting tighter, will they manage to elude their terrible pursuers? This book by Susan Schade and Jon Buller is a lot of fun, and we're sure you'll love it!

DISNEY GRAPHIC NOVELS - An all-new graphic novel series, as the name clearly states, that features a rotating line-up of major Disney stars. In the first volume, PLANES are featured, but for all you cartoon mouse lovers, none other than Mickey Mouse himself stars in the second volume! In a series called X-MICKEY, he explores all sorts of supernatural happenings.

ut the biggest news of all may not be on the Papercutz website. As some of you may know, the GERONIMO STILTON and HEA STILTON graphic novels have been produced in Italy and translated and published in English by Papercutz. Starting ith THEA STILTON #5, we're now producing the THEA STILTON and GERONIMO STILTON graphic novels ourselves from e start! Well, Geronimo and Thea will still be telling their stories to writers Francesco Savino and Leonardo Favia, who will rite their scripts in Italian, and Nanette McGuinness will still translate it all into English, but now Editor Carol Burrell and ssociate Editor Bethany Bryan will put the comics together working with artist Ryan Jampole, colorists Mindy Indy and yjay Jackson, and letterers Wilson Ramos, Jr. and Grace Lu. We think we've managed to maintain the style you've come to ve, and we're eager to hear what you think. Please send your feedback to the addresses listed below.

o, until we meet again in THEA STILTON #6, e sure not to miss GERONIMO STILTON #16 *ights, Camera, Stilton!* Check out the preview n the following pages.

hanks,

Jim

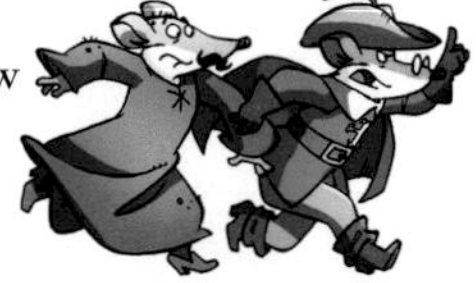

Stay in Touch!

Email: Papercutz@papercutz.com
Web: www.papercutz.com
Twitter: @papercutzgn
Facebook: PAPERCUTZGRAPHICNOVELS
Snailmail: Papercutz, 160 Broadway, Suite 700, East Wing, New York, NY 10038

Special Preview of GERONIMO STILTON #16 "Lights, Camera, Stilton!"

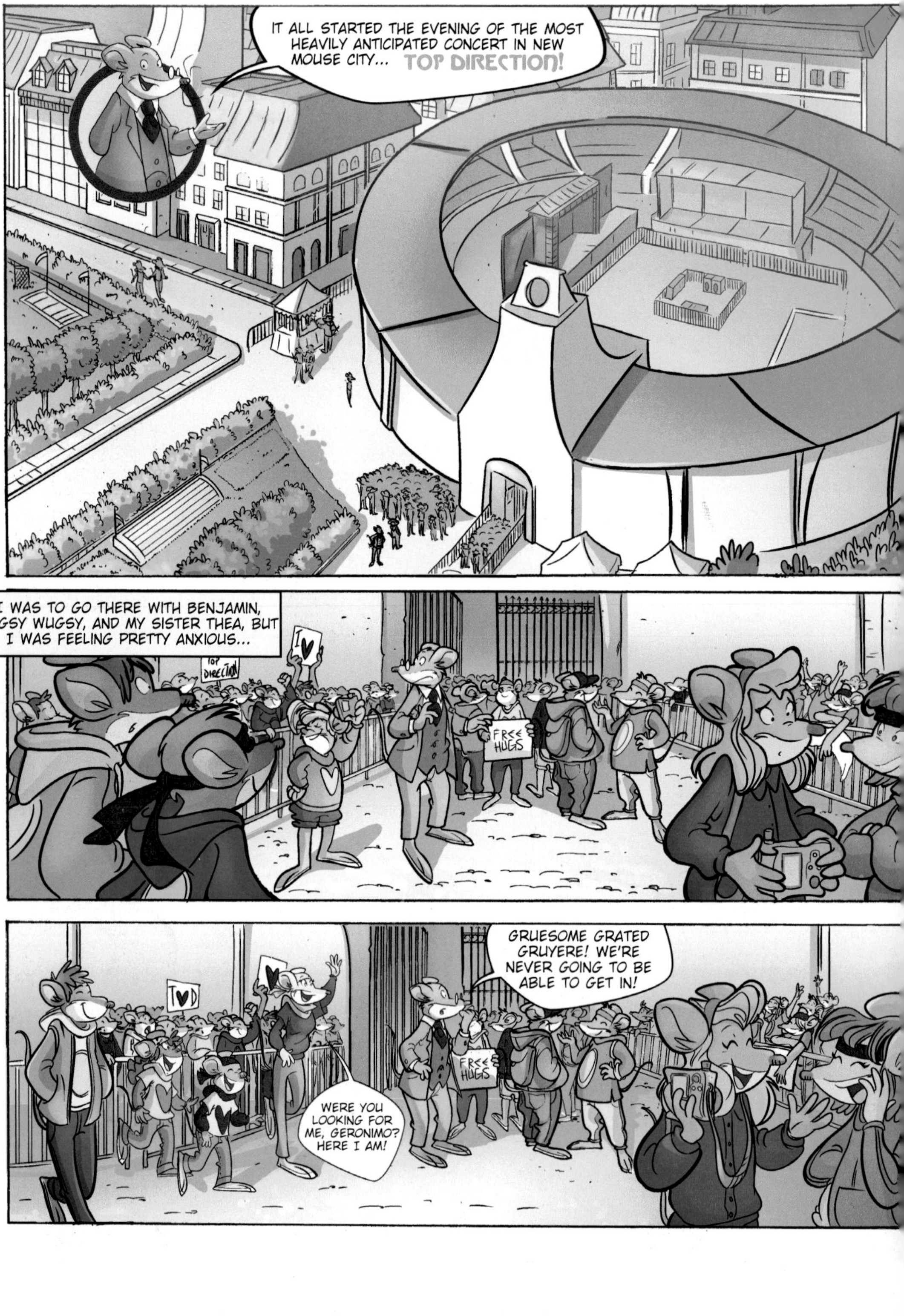
IT ALL STARTED THE EVENING OF THE MOST HEAVILY ANTICIPATED CONCERT IN NEW MOUSE CITY... TOP DIRECTION!
I WAS TO GO THERE WITH BENJAMIN, BUGSY WUGSY, AND MY SISTER THEA, BUT I WAS FEELING PRETTY ANXIOUS...
TOP DIRECTION
FREE HUGS
GRUESOME GRATED GRUYERE! WE'RE NEVER GOING TO BE ABLE TO GET IN!
FREE HUGS
WERE YOU LOOKING FOR ME, GERONIMO? HERE I AM!

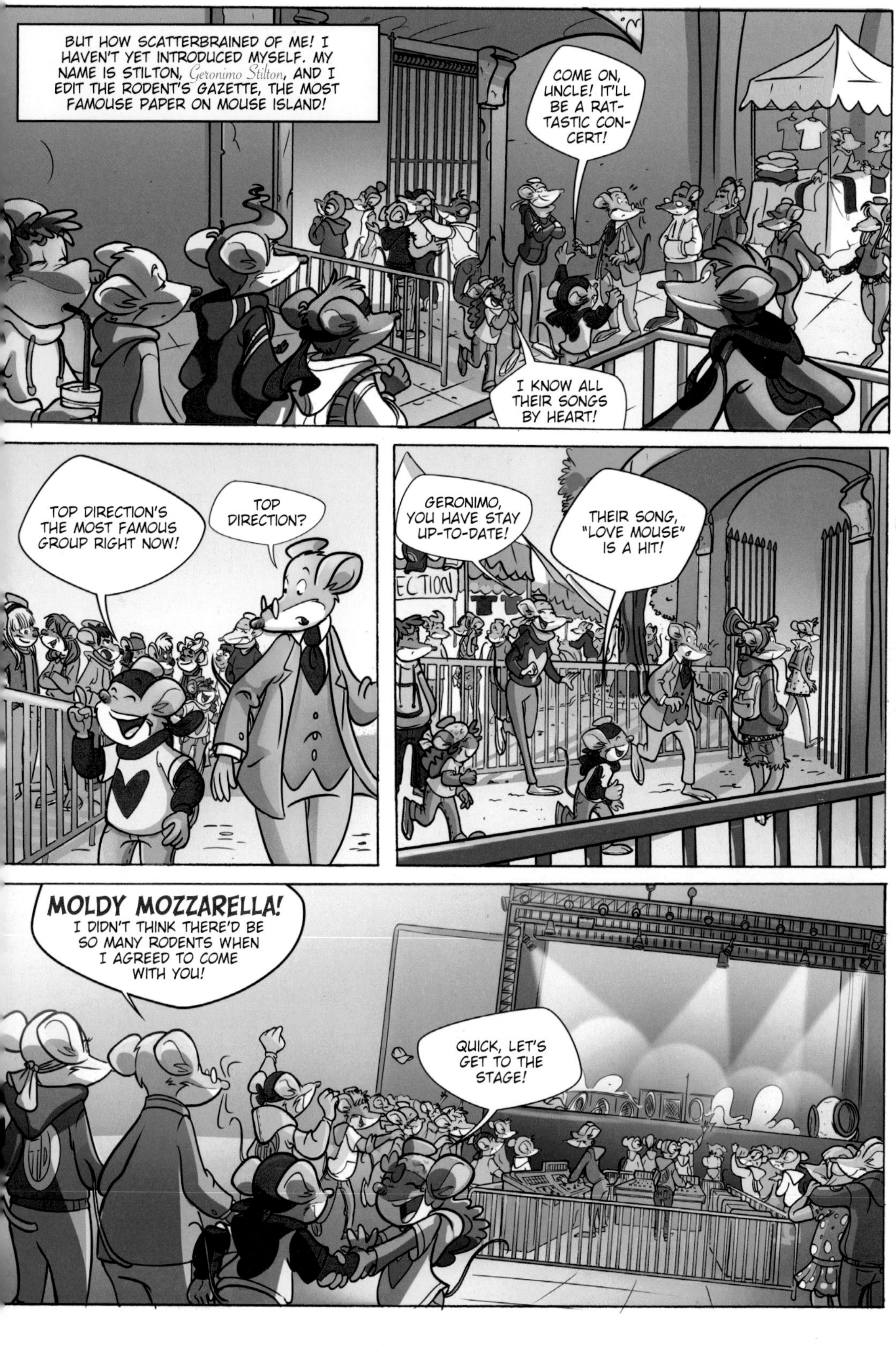
BUT HOW SCATTERBRAINED OF ME! I HAVEN'T YET INTRODUCED MYSELF. MY NAME IS STILTON, Geronimo Stilton, AND I EDIT THE RODENT'S GAZETTE, THE MOST FAMOUSE PAPER ON MOUSE ISLAND!
COME ON, UNCLE! IT'LL BE A RAT-TASTIC CONCERT!
I KNOW ALL THEIR SONGS BY HEART!
TOP DIRECTION'S THE MOST FAMOUS GROUP RIGHT NOW!
TOP DIRECTION?
GERONIMO, YOU HAVE STAY UP-TO-DATE!
THEIR SONG, "LOVE MOUSE" IS A HIT!
ECTION
MOLDY MOZZARELLA!
I DIDN'T THINK THERE'D BE SO MANY RODENTS WHEN I AGREED TO COME WITH YOU!
QUICK, LET'S GET TO THE STAGE!

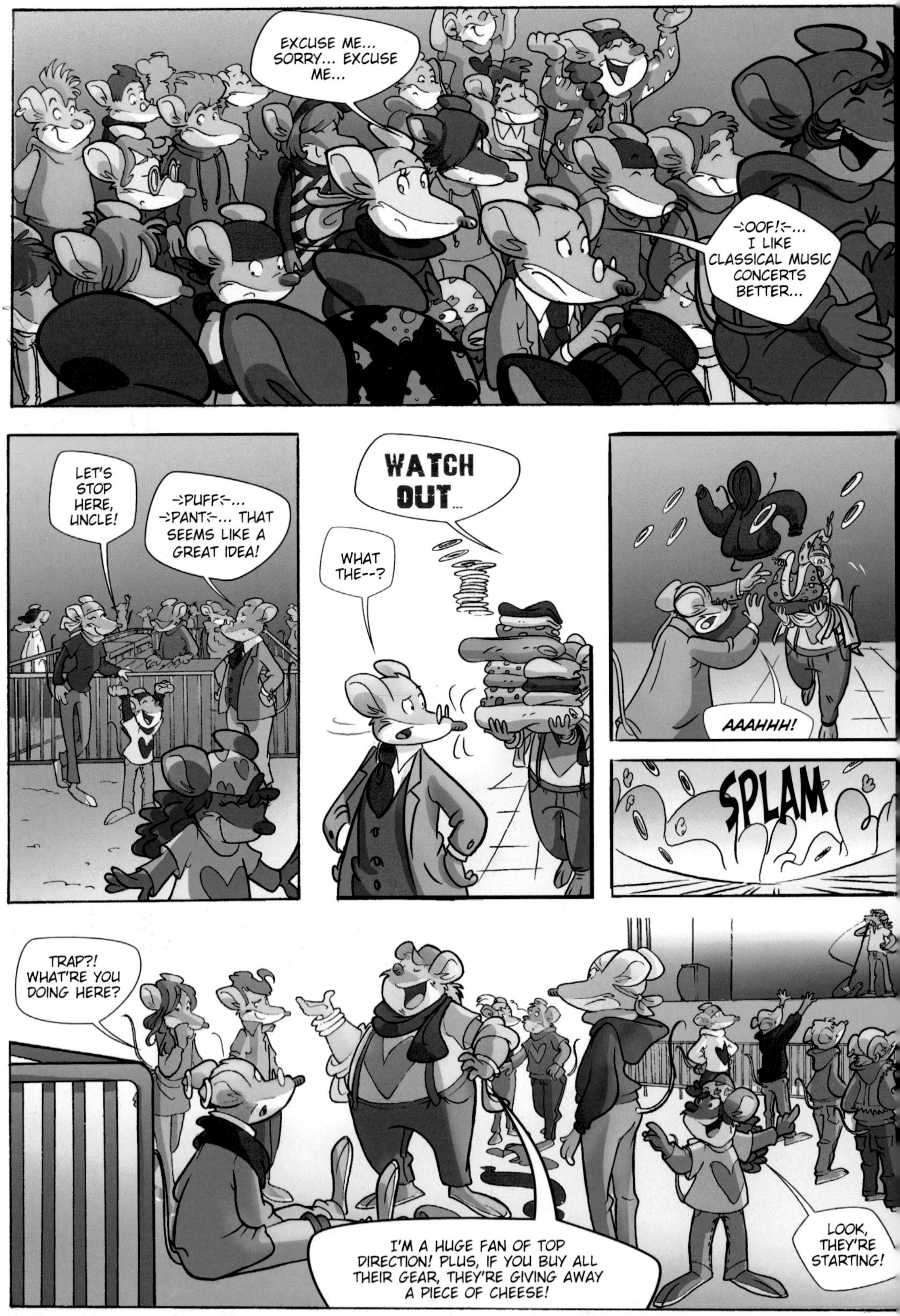
EXCUSE ME... SORRY... EXCUSE ME...
-OOF!-... I LIKE CLASSICAL MUSIC CONCERTS BETTER...
LET'S STOP HERE, UNCLE!
-PUFF-... -PANT-... THAT SEEMS LIKE A GREAT IDEA!
WATCH OUT...
WHAT THE--?
AAAHHH!
SPLAM
TRAP?! WHAT'RE YOU DOING HERE?
I'M A HUGE FAN OF TOP DIRECTION! PLUS, IF YOU BUY ALL THEIR GEAR, THEY'RE GIVING AWAY A PIECE OF CHEESE!
LOOK, THEY'RE STARTING!

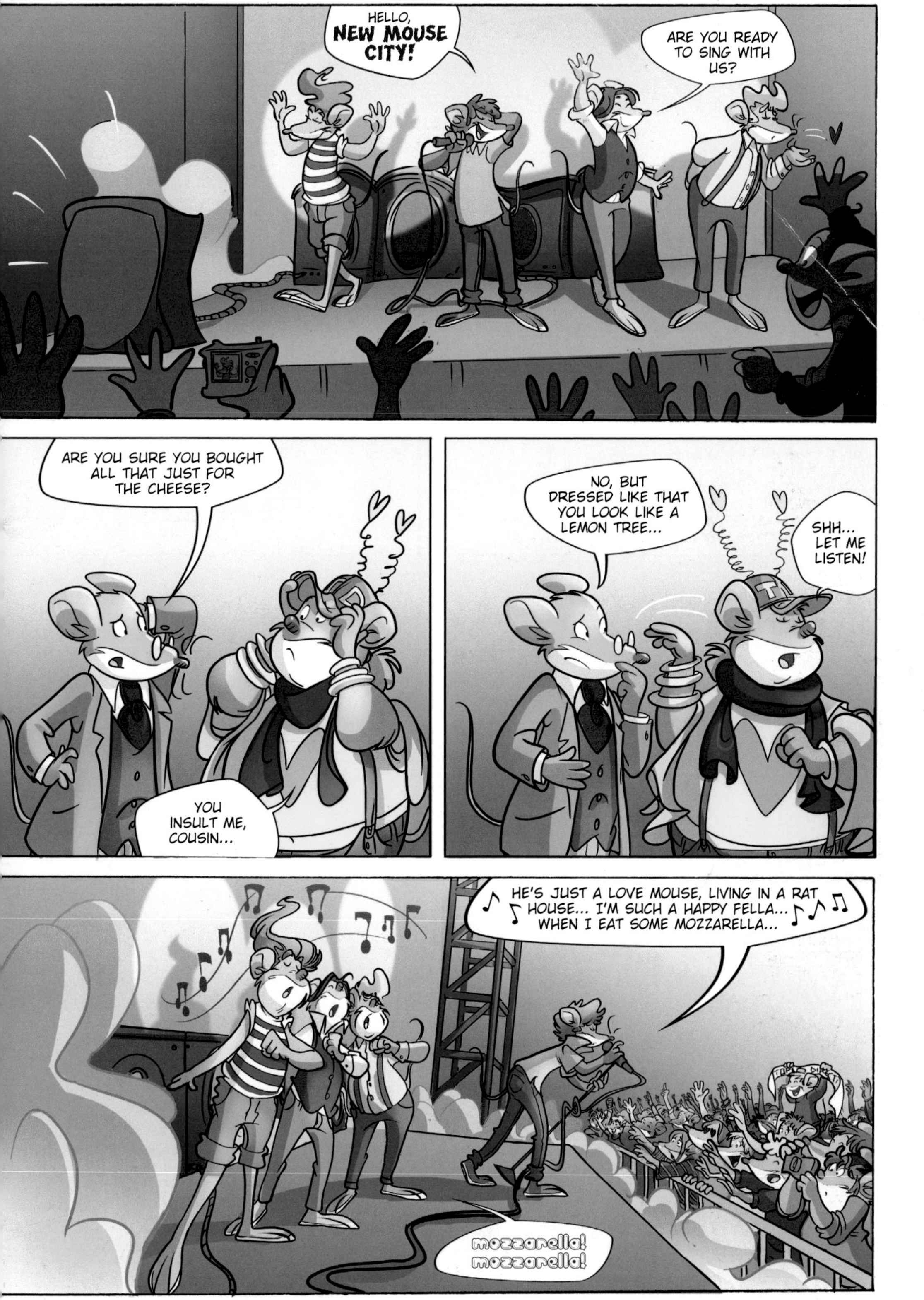
HELLO, NEW MOUSE CITY!
ARE YOU READY TO SING WITH US?
ARE YOU SURE YOU BOUGHT ALL THAT JUST FOR THE CHEESE?
YOU INSULT ME, COUSIN...
NO, BUT DRESSED LIKE THAT YOU LOOK LIKE A LEMON TREE...
SHH... LET ME LISTEN!
HE'S JUST A LOVE MOUSE, LIVING IN A RAT HOUSE... I'M SUCH A HAPPY FELLA... WHEN I EAT SOME MOZZARELLA...
mozzarella! mozzarella!

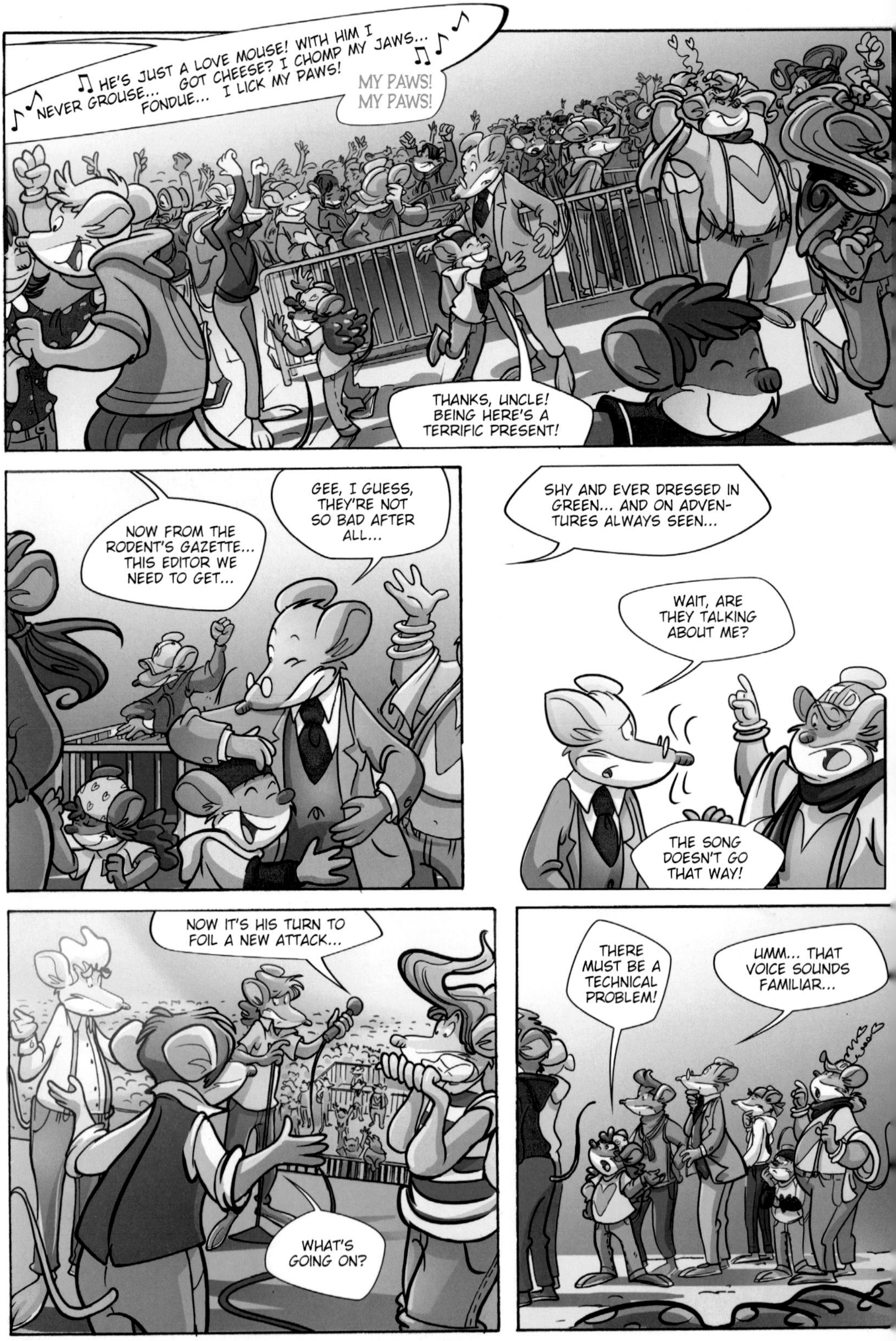
HE'S JUST A LOVE MOUSE! WITH HIM I NEVER GROUSE... GOT CHEESE? I CHOMP MY JAWS... FONDUE... I LICK MY PAWS!
MY PAWS! MY PAWS!
THANKS, UNCLE! BEING HERE'S A TERRIFIC PRESENT!
NOW FROM THE RODENT'S GAZETTE... THIS EDITOR WE NEED TO GET...
GEE, I GUESS, THEY'RE NOT SO BAD AFTER ALL...
SHY AND EVER DRESSED IN GREEN... AND ON ADVENTURES ALWAYS SEEN...
WAIT, ARE THEY TALKING ABOUT ME?
THE SONG DOESN'T GO THAT WAY!
NOW IT'S HIS TURN TO FOIL A NEW ATTACK...
WHAT'S GOING ON?
THERE MUST BE A TECHNICAL PROBLEM!
UMM... THAT VOICE SOUNDS FAMILIAR...

Don't Miss GERONIMO STILTON #16 "Lights, Camera, Stilton!"